STELLA'S VERY SPECIAL SUMMER

STELLA'S VERY SPECIAL SUMMER

Carol Lunney-Hampson

Table of Contents

Dedication i

Prologue ii

One 1

Two 11

Three 19

Four 27

Five 33

Six 41

Seven 47

Eight 53

Nine 65

Ten 71

Eleven 81

Twelve 91

Thirteen 99

Fourteen 115

Fifteen 123

Sixteen 131

Seventeen 141

Recipes 145

Acknowledgments 146

About the Author 147

Questions for Discussion 148

DEDICATION

To my father Fritz and my mother Bertha who provided me with the priceless gift of a childhood on the river. This fueled my own sustained love of nature which I passed on to my son Michael

To my brother Frankie who did get to fly

Also, to my grandsons Victor and Sebastian and to my grand-niece Quinn—with the hope they will read this story and learn more about their grandmothers' childhoods

Finally, to my godson, John, who adored his grandfather Poppy Fritz and kept the tradition with his own cabin on the edge of the water in Kentucky for many years.

PROLOGUE

Pounding rain beats against a glass door leading to our deck that faces the now angry creek; gusts of wind tangle branches of loblolly pine trees above a swirling and flooded yard. Hurricane Florence, September 14, 2018, hits the North Carolina coast with unparalleled fury.

I peer through the window to see our creek has risen to cover the dock and lower level of a two-tiered garden. At this rate of rising, it will soon reach the bottom floor of our house.

We decided to wait-out the storm and watch over our retirement investment, our house, and boats. The surge was predicted to be nine feet, but it is almost to that point now and still rising. It will flood at least another few feet according to the weather experts.

We think we will be fine since the living space is built on pilings twelve feet high, but I shiver uncontrollably as I recall the memories of another hurricane almost seventy years ago.

* * *

The summer of 1955 was full of all the magical moments and tragic events that can mold the character of an eleven-year-old girl.

It was a time in our country when cell phones and laptops didn't exist, telephones were big black devices with hard-wired party lines. Black and white televisions were just starting to appear in family households. Summer vacations started the day school let out in June and ended on Labor Day.

Polio was still widespread across the country. This paralyzing disease had already killed over 6,000 children and although the newly approved Salk vaccine appeared to be effective, the disease seemed more prevalent in the summer months. Parents were cautious about their children being exposed at swimming pools and some beaches, so this disease was proving disastrous for water-based businesses.

This was a critical summer for the Karvotsky family. The fish camp business on the edge of a river in the northeast Catskill Mountains provided the extra financial support that was desperately needed to supplement the family's income.

Share this period of Stella's childhood as she takes you on a most educational tour of a tween's summer vacation dealing with friendships and responsibilities. It is a very special, yet potentially tragic, summer.

ONE

Getting Out of Town

The bell clanged outside Stella's fifth-grade classroom at St. Victoria's Catholic School and shocked her out of a daydream. Her dream, as usual, involved the Cabin at the river and a beautiful white horse.

This year her mother had promised Stella she could try to swim across the whole river for the first time.

Another hope for this summer was once they got to the Cabin, Stella could figure out how to meet the red-haired girl and her big white horse she had seen riding on River Road last fall. Stella thought, this could be a very special summer!

She jumped out of her seat before the bell's clanging ended and shouted down the aisle to her best friend Helen.

"Finally! I thought that bell would never stop." Stella grabbed her brown canvas book bag and was the first student to the door. Sister Gerry had given Stella a bundle of books related to horses to read during the summer, and earlier she had packed these into her bag to save time.

Impatient, she yelled to her friend, "Hurry up, Helen."

Helen stumbled past the desks, frustrated with Stella's orders. "I'm hurrying already. Hold onto your pants!"

Sister Gerry stationed herself at the classroom door for her students goodbyes.

"Have a good summer, Stella, and congratulations on getting the highest class average this year. I know you worked hard for it." Sister Gerry hugged Stella, then Helen.

She lowered her starched headpiece toward them and sternly said, "You girls be sure to go to Mass every Sunday."

Stella and Helen, careful to avoid direct eye contact with Sister Gerry, quickly nodded their response to her. Stella nudged Helen out the door and turned.

"Bye, Sister Gerry. Thanks for the books. I can hardly wait to start reading Black Beauty. You have a good summer too."

But Stella thought, I'm not making any promises about church EVERY Sunday. Once out the door, they high fived each other and together ran down the hall.

"No running, you girlies." Happy the janitor yelled at Stella and Helen as he opened the main doors for the oncoming herd of children.

The girls stopped running and slowed down to a fast walk. "Sorry, Happy. Hope you have a good summer."

"No worries about that," Happy responded with a wave of his hand. "There's plenty of fish right here in the Lackawaxen to catch." Then he exploded with his signature laugh.

This put the girls into their own laughing spell as they skipped down the steps. Stella rearranged her book bag on her shoulder. "Yeah! No more homework for three whole months."

Outside the school, they waited at the curb. Stella impatiently tapped her Buster Brown shoe and twirled a shock of blonde straight hair at the back of her head. The school guard waved a big yellow bus to pass.

"Now, let's go!" Stella urged her friend to cross, and they ran past the rectory and convent where the priests and nuns lived. They slowed to a walk in front of the huge purple granite church, blessed themselves hurriedly, "In name of Father, Son, Holy Ghost," and turned into the dirt alley at the corner.

They ran past the concrete stoop at the back of the grocery store where all their friends usually hung out after school and on weekends. Stella could not afford the time to chat today, so she told Helen, "Boy, I'm sure going to miss everybody, but you'll have to write and give me the news, okay?"

"Don't worry, Stel." Helen said, out of breath from running. "I'll keep you up to date." Helen was a little pudgy, and she was struggling with Stella's pace.

Further up the hilly dirt road, Stella noticed the neighbor's lilac bush was nearly blossomed out.

"You know, lilacs are my favorite flowers. Don't you think this is the biggest bush in the world?" It shaded most of the alley. "When it's in full bloom, I can smell lilacs all the way in my backyard!"

At the top of the hill, panting from carrying the heavy bookbag, Stella stopped next to her family's empty chicken coop. She took a few deep breaths, waiting for Helen to catch up. She pinched her nose and thought, "Hmm, that chicken poop is still so smelly."

When her friend finally walked up, breathing heavily, and dragging her bookbag, Stella said, "Well, Helen, have a good summer here in the hot city. Remember, you said you'd come up the Cabin and spend a week with me. Our mamas agreed, and my daddy said he could bring you one weekend and take you back the next one, okay?"

"Yeah, when I find out the week my folks will let me go, I'll write you. Boy, I'm going to miss you, Stel." Helen dropped her bag and faced Stella. They shared a long hug, but Stella had to break away because she felt a knot forming in her throat.

Helen turned and wiped away tears, picked up her bookbag, then shuffled down the alley toward her house a few backyards away.

Stella ran back to the center of the alley, cupped her mouth with both hands and yelled. "Bye, Helen-melon. See you up the Cabin!" Helen turned, and the friends waved to each other one last time.

* * *

Stella walked between her family's garage and the rundown chicken coop, dragging her book bag across the bumpy, coal-ash driveway.

A blonde fuzzy mongrel ran up the yard from the house to greet her, ears flying and tail whirling like a propeller. He tried to jump on her.

"Down, Peppy!" Stella stooped down and hugged his furry neck. "Ready to go?"

Peppy jumped back and barked as though he understood, then led the way across the lawn to the back of the house, where a 1950 two-tone gray Chevy was parked right next to the back steps of the clapboard duplex. The open trunk of the car was filled with food, clothes, bedding, and kitchen supplies, enough for a family with four kids and a dog for three months.

Wow, Mama has filled the trunk already. Thank you, God, now Peppy can ride inside the car with us. Stella hated it when on some trips, Peppy had to ride in the trunk and she worried the whole time, even though her father always said it wouldn't hurt him for an hour or so.

She opened the driver's side door, threw her book bag on the back floorboards, and skipped up the wooden steps of the house. The screen door on the porch slammed behind her as she ran through the kitchen and up the wooden staircase to her tiny room.

She changed from the school uniform she hated into soft, worn jeans and a sweatshirt.

"Bye, room." Stella scanned her bed and desk for any last items. Then, as a final gesture, she pulled her desk lamp plug from the wall. "See you on Labor Day!"

* * *

Stella was skipping down the stairs from her bedroom when her brother Harry slammed the screen door and strutted into the kitchen. He was only two years older, but often acted many years wiser.

"I am ready to go," she announced as she pulled her shoulders back and strutted over to her brother.

"Okay! OOKAY!" He put his hands on his hips and threw his slender shoulders back. "So, you beat me home. Big deal. But don't think you're riding up front."

He wagged a menacing finger in Stella's face, grabbed her in a neck hold, and scrambled her long blonde hair. "Shotgun is reserved for me and Peppy."

Stella pushed him away and smoothed her tangled hair. "As if I cared," she said. "I just want to get there."

"Stella, Harry, are you both home?" Their mother called from the bottom of the backdoor steps. They both went onto the back porch to greet her.

"Mama, Mama, guess what. I DID get the highest average in class! You should have seen the look on Barb Oleski's face. She missed it by two points. Boy, she was upset."

Mama climbed the steps and gave Stella a hug. "Stel, that's great. We're all proud of you."

Stella turned to her brother, "And that jerk Eddie, he tripped me in the aisle when I went to get my report card from Father John. I nearly fell on my face."

Harry harrumphed, slapping his fist into his open hand. "Don't worry. I'll get him back next fall, maybe one day at recess. Then I'll remind him why he got beat up." They both started laughing and carrying on, but their mother interrupted.

"Stop that, both of you. Listen, I put your suitcases in the car. Harry, help me get these last things packed, and Stella, wake up the twins from their nap. Get them to the bathroom and dressed. I put their clothes on their beds. We need to get there before dark."

"Okay, Mama." She turned and gave Harry an unexpected punch on his arm, laughed, and ran into the house before he could catch her.

She went back upstairs and tiptoed into the bedroom where the twins were asleep. They would turn four this summer and were a handful. Her mother trusted Stella as their babysitter. After all, she'd be twelve this fall.

Most times, Stella didn't mind babysitting. She enjoyed playing mama to them. But sometimes, when her friends went off without her, she felt cheated because she'd rather be playing kickball in the alley than staying home wiping snotty noses.

Stella wondered again how they could be called twins when one was a boy and one was a girl, and they did not look alike. Mama said it had to do with eggs, but Stella didn't understand.

She thought, "we're supposed to learn science next year in school. I might figure it out then."

Stella patted her little brother Stanley on his back and cooed in his ear to try and gently awaken him. She didn't want him waking up screaming. Stanley was his baptized name, but even at three he hated it, and everybody called him Stosh.

"Stosh, time to get up." she whispered. His light brown hair was longer than their daddy liked, but their mother said it was so curly and cute she hated to cut it. Now, it was plastered against his face with sweat.

He rolled over and smiled, and then belly-laughed when he saw Stella making google-eyes at him.

"Hi, Stosh, did you have a good nap? I'm going to wake up Elsie and get you two dressed so we can get on the road. You remember where we're going?"

"Yep!" he said, matter-of-factly. "Up the Cabin."

"Good. Now go potty while I get your clothes ready. You want help?"

"Nah, I'm a big boy now. He padded out of the bedroom and down the hall.

Stella tiptoed to the other twin bed. "Elllssieee," she sing-songed in her little sister's ear. Elsie's curly hair was deep brown, almost black, like her father's side of the family. She opened her dark brown eyes and blinked. Elsie had the longest eyelashes, and Stella was almost jealous of them since her own were blonde and skimpy.

"Come on, Princess. Time to wake up. Mama's waiting."

Elsie whined a bit, but Stella managed to get her out of bed, to the bathroom, and into her clothes.

"Stella, I'm stuck!" Stosh yelled from the bedroom. He was trying to get his head and one arm through the neckband of his shirt. Stella laughed and helped him finish and they all raced down the staircase to the kitchen.

After a snack of cold apple juice and graham crackers, Stella corralled the twins toward the car where her mother and Harry were waiting for them. Peppy shadowed Harry's every move, not wanting to be forgotten in case there was a ride in his future.

Her father came out of the garage to see them off. He cleaned black stuff off his hands as he walked toward them.

"He must've been working on his truck's engine again," Stella thought.

Last week, she overheard a conversation between her father and mother about an overdue bank loan for the Cabin. Fred said he wished they could afford a new truck for his bread-delivery route but told Sophie it wasn't in the cards unless they did a really good business at the Fish Camp this summer.

Fred looked at the over-packed trunk, shook his head in disbelief, and smiled as he stuffed the greasy rag into the back pocket of his coveralls.

Stella knew he was only a few years older than her mother, but she thought he looked much older. The afternoon sun highlighted the furrows on his brow and around his dark eyes. Though, except for his silver sideburns, his hair was still dark and shiny. Stella thought her father was very handsome.

He told her mother, "Sophie, if you have trouble turning on the electricity, I wrote instructions inside the breaker panel. And Harry can manage turning on the water. I showed him how when we were up there a few weeks ago. And don't forget, Mr. Ward's coming tomorrow morning early to rent one of our cabins, two boats and a motor for the weekend. I signed them up in the book for Cabin Two."

"Yes, Fred," her mother answered slowly, smiling but sounding exasperated.

Her father turned to face her brother. "Harry, put the 5 Horsepower Evinrude motor on No. 1 boat tonight and start it, so there's no problem tomorrow. And remind those guys where the rapids are, so you don't have to tow them back."

Then he turned and focused on Stella. "Stella, remember that Harry and I turned those boats over on the riverbank and put them in the water two weeks ago, so make sure you clean them up real good and check for leaks."

Stella quickly replied, "Okay, Daddy, I'll make sure they're ready."

Harry and her father shared a manly hug. Then Harry walked to the passenger side with Peppy close on his heels. He opened the door to let the dog jump in ahead of him.

Stella coaxed the twins into the backseat, climbed in, and sat between them so they wouldn't fight.

Finally, her mother got into the car, slammed the door, and rolled down the window. Her father walked around the car, kicked the tires, and closed the trunk. Sophie rested her head against the window frame.

"I must be crazy," she told Fred. "Here I am again, taking four kids and a dog up into the woods. Fred Karvotsky, you got lucky this go round!"

"Sorry, Sophie," her father drew out the "sorry" part and laughed. "I'll be there tomorrow as soon as I can. You'll be all right. Harry knows our start up routine." He winked at his son in the front seat.

"Call me tonight, Sophie. The phone should be working by the time you get there."

"Oh Fred, don't forget those boxes I left in the living room. We'll need them, okay?"

"Sure, as long as you don't want me to bring the kitchen sink, too," her father laughed.

"Oh, never mind," her mother said, forcing a smile.

"I wish she loved the Cabin half as much as me," Stella thought. She knew her mother wasn't exactly thrilled about going there, especially without her daddy.

When Sophie turned on the ignition, the engine started, but a puff of smoke shot out the tailpipe.

Fred stared at the back of the car with a puzzled look on his face, shook his head, then slapped the side of the car. "Bye, honeybuns, see you tomorrow."

Then with a stern expression on his face, he poked his head into the car, glancing for a moment at each of his children, and said, "Look, you kids be good and listen to Ma." Stosh and Elsie just lowered their heads.

He stepped away and his demeanor changed. Jokingly he said, "Oh, Sophie, watch your speed in Coalville because they need money to build a new Town Hall."

"You know I do not speed. You're the one that better watch out!" her mother retorted. She pushed in the clutch, shifted into first gear, and slowly pulled out of the driveway.

They drove into the dirt alley and down the hill Stella and Helen had just run up. At the bottom, when her mother honked the horn twice, everybody turned and waved to their daddy, who was still standing in the middle of the alley at the top of the hill. He waved back.

When they passed the old purple granite church, everyone crossed themselves in unison. Stella chuckled to herself at the intensity of the twins attempts at the sign of the cross.

As they passed the school, Stella saw Happy sweeping the front steps. They all yelled, "Hi, Happy!" and he waved back. Stella thought she could make out his special laugh.

She felt a twinge of sadness leaving the city and her friends, but thoughts of the summer ahead made the sadness fly away.

The car chugged up the winding, narrow, one-mile hill out of the valley. Stella pulled the new copy of Black Beauty out of her bag. She examined the cover and traced the outline of the horse with her finger. "I can hardly wait to start reading you," she whispered. She put the book back in her bag and pulled out another well-worn book.

"Ok, guys. Want me to read Tales of Peter Rabbit?"

"Yes, yes," the twins chimed. Stella hoped it wouldn't be long before the story put them back asleep.

At the top of the valley, the road met the main highway that would lead them into the mountains.

Stella lay back against the seat and sighed. Finally, we're on our way up the Cabin!

TWO

On The Way

They were all glad to be on the road. There wasn't much traffic, and Stella's mother hoped to get through Coalville before the five o'clock rush. It was only an hour-and-a-half trip, but with the twins, there would have to be at least one potty stop.

For the past week, her mother had nearly driven Stella crazy with all her worrying about what to take for the summer. She kept reminding Stella and Harry to get their clothes ready. By Wednesday, Stella had her suitcase packed. Then she helped her mother collect what the twins needed and all the food, including jars of homemade preserves, canned fruits, and veggies.

The first week at the Cabin was always the toughest. Even though her mother had done this routine for the past six years, she always forgot something - a roasting pan, extra pillows, jackets for the kids.

I wonder what it will be this time, Stella thought. At least the twins were out of their stupid diapers. And her mother could always drive the mile into town to grocery shop.

"Rats!" Her mother thumped the steering wheel with her fist. "I left the tapioca pudding in the refrigerator. Sorry, Harry, that was our dessert for tonight." She patted Harry's shoulder. "I know it's your favorite. And I made it with pineapple, too."

Harry, his voice sounding more like her father's, laughed, "Ah, don't worry about it, Ma, when we call Dad tonight, we'll tell him to bring it for tomorrow's dinner."

Stella laughed to herself. *So, it's the tapioca pudding she forgot this time. Not so bad.*

She sat back in the seat and listened to the radio. Since Harry was in front, he got to pick the station, and the song "Melody of Love" was playing. It was a new singer called Billy Vaughn. Sister Gerry said she liked Billy Vaughn's music, but she was not a fan of the newest singer called Elvis.

She said he was a bad influence on young people because he wiggled his hips too much.

Stella thought about what her first dance would be like and had one more year to find out. The seventh, eighth, and ninth graders had a dance every month at school, except during Lent, and this was Harry's first year to go. He went to most of the dance parties.

Stella tried to get all the details, but he was closed mouth about it and said it was no big deal. She knew he was stuck on Theresa Lipinski and wondered if they had danced to "Melody of Love."

Stella remembered that after one dance Harry brought Terry back home, and they sat on the swing under the budka in the backyard. The budka is a three-sided trellis with a roof and grape vines growing through the wood slats, so it's pretty secluded.

But Stella spied on them from the bathroom window and saw Harry give Terry one whopping kiss on the cheek! Even though she knew they couldn't see her, Stella felt her face flush hot and afterwards felt so guilty, she didn't spy anymore.

Stella glanced over at the twins, happy they were asleep. She was only half-way through Peter Rabbit when she saw Stosh's eyes closing and Elsie leaning against her.

Peace and quiet, she thought. Then she rested her head on the backseat and daydreamed.

* * *

She thought about the Cabin a lot during the winter months. When it snowed at home in the valley, she pictured the Cabin nestled in the mountains in a white gown with royal-blue window eyelets.

This past February, on George Washington's Birthday, her father decided to take everyone on a day trip to see how things were up there.

It was the coldest day this winter, and Stella remembered the bare black walnut tree with a few nuts still clinging to branches when they pulled into the snow-covered driveway.

With the blinds all drawn, the Cabin was cold and dark, and the floor creaked as they walked from room to room. Inside, it was so cold you could blow smoke from your breath.

"Hey, look Stel, I'm smoking!" Harry pretended he was holding a cigarette and blew "smoke" into the air.

Stella longed to make a fire, but her father said it was too much trouble for a couple of hours. Instead, he turned on the propane gas heater in the living room and cracked all the other doors for venting.

Everyone had to pee in the outhouse because the water pipes had been drained for the winter. Her mother brought ham sandwiches with lettuce and mayonnaise and hot sweet tea with lemon.

While the family sat around the big round oak pedestal table in the warm living room to eat their picnic lunch, Stella took hers outside. She brushed snow from the swing seat under the black walnut tree and sat down. The view took her breath away.

The Cabin sat on the snow-covered riverbank, and the river was frozen everywhere except for a ten-foot wide slit at its very center. The wooden fishing boats lay upside down along the bank and were covered with snow.

A bright warm sun reflected rainbows off the snow and ice, so Stella felt as if she were inside a kaleidoscope, just like the one she got last Christmas in her stocking. She remembered its multicolored sparkling reflections.

The surrounding sounds were so clear. She could hear the echo of the water rushing through a narrow channel of unfrozen water at the surface of the river, the melting ice dripping like a symphony from the trees and roof of the Cabin, and the occasional caw-caw of a distant crow.

* * *

"Stella, we're coming into Coalville. Are the twins still asleep?"

At the sound of her mother's voice, Stella snapped out of her reverie.

"Yeah, Mama," she answered. "Sure makes the trip quieter without their yapping. Stella, why is the sky blue? Stella, why are there lines on the road? Glad they're going to school next year so they can find out for themselves."

"My dear, you asked those same questions," her mother cast a knowing look backward before she maneuvered the car through a series of detours on the outskirts of Coalville. Piles of coal slag lined the temporary road on both sides.

"Looks like they're still trying to put out the fire that started in the mine shafts," Harry broke in. "Can you believe they tore down the Esso station that was right here when Dad and I came through two weeks ago? Dad thinks they're going to have to move the whole town before it's all done."

"Whew, Harry, roll up your window, pu-leez!" Stella pinched her nose. The smell of sulfur and smoke made her eyes water. "How can people live here?"

"Well, some people just don't have a choice," her mother said, still focused on the winding road.

After leaving Coalville, the road to the Cabin was pretty much uphill through the country. Going past the reservoir, Stella noticed the rhododendrons on the shady side of the lake were blooming.

They passed the apple orchards where they had bought fresh squeezed cider last fall.

Stella remembered the sweet, fruity smell in the cider house, the sound of apples bouncing toward the press, and the crunching as the press squeezed the amber juice from the fruit. Now, the orchard was purely pink with blossoms.

"Look at those blossoms!" Sophie exclaimed, "Most of the trees have already set fruit. If nothing bad happens weather-wise, this is going to be another good year for apples."

Elsie began squirming awake. "Stella, I'm thirsty. Can I have a drink?" she whined.

"Mama, Elsie's up and she's thirsty," Stella announced, not sure what to do.

Almost on cue, Stosh opened his eyes. "Stella, I have to pee."

Stella sighed. "Mama, now we got one thirsty and one to pee. How long before we stop?"

"About ten minutes, honey. We'll stop at Fern Lake Grill for gas and ice cream. Sound good to everybody?"

"Ice Cream! Ice Cream!" The twins yelled in unison.

Peppy jumped up, dazed from his nap on the front seat, to see whether the ruckus meant he had to protect or play with the riders.

Soon Sophie pulled into the front parking lot of the Grill. Fern Lake was a summer resort, but the crowds had not yet arrived. Only a few locals were parked in the lot.

Most of the vacationers came from New York City or big towns in New Jersey. Stella thought they talked funny, especially when they pronounced "water" as "wadda."

Sometimes they came to the Fish Camp to rent boats even though Fern Lake had their own boats and canoes for rent. She knew it was the beauty of the river that brought them.

Harry let out a low whistle, "Wow, Ma! Gas went up five cents from two weeks ago. It was nineteen cents a gallon when Dad and I filled up. They must be getting ready for the city folks."

Sophie just shook her head. After she pulled the car up to the gas pump and shut off the engine, she said, "Okay, now remember, this must be a short stop. Stella, you take the twins to the bathroom. Make sure they wash their hands."

While Stella took the twins around the back of the grill, Harry filled the car with gas and helped his mother bring out the ice cream. They all sat on the long wooden bench beneath a red neon sign that flashed "OPEN."

When his mother wasn't looking, Harry let Peppy have a couple of licks of ice cream from his cone. Stella helped clean up Stosh and Elsie's sticky hands and then they all piled back in the car.

A few miles past Fern Lake, the family always played a game to see who spotted Mr. Gannett's big red barn first. Sometimes, if Stella were daydreaming, she would miss it, but today she focused.

Just as her mother started to round the curve, Stella yelled, jumping up and down on the backseat, "I see Gannett's. I see the red barn!" Harry turned around, looking disgusted, and stuck his tongue out at her.

Then the twins started jumping up and down on the seat yelling, "Stella won! Stella won!"

Sophie slowed as they passed the barn so they could see Mr. Gannett's two old workhorses, Tom and Ginny.

Tom was a steel-gray gelding Percheron, and his head was almost as big as Peppy's whole body. Each foot was the size of a small dinner plate, but he was very gentle.

Ginny was a dappled, light gray mare, slightly smaller than Tom, and very much in love with him. Wherever Tom was, Ginny was. The two horses had worked together since they were young, and Stella thought Mr. Gannett treated them like they were his children.

Today he was standing in a corral next to the barn feeding the horses a pile of hay. Mr. Gannett wore blue faded coveralls and his trademark big black hat. Sophie slowed down and honked twice, and Mr. Gannett took off his hat and waved to them with it.

The children yelled out the windows in unison, "Hello, Mr. Gannett," and waved until the car turned the bend and Mr. Gannett, his horses, and the red barn disappeared. The family had no way of knowing this would be the last time they could play this game.

From here on, the trip was chaos. Everybody talked at the same time and pointed out landmarks. They passed Spooky Road where they went for hayrides on summer evenings, and Stella pointed out the Haunted House up on the hill. Past a clearing of thick pine trees, the river came into view on the right.

"They must've had a lot of rain upstream this week because the river really looks high today," Harry commented, with a tone of concern.

Right before the main road met the Darbytown Bridge that crossed the river, Sophie slowed down.

Harry's father and his buddies had made a sign and planted it right before the bridge, "Fish Camp, 1 mile" and an arrow pointing left.

Sophie followed the arrow's direction and took a sharp left onto River Road.

Here, the overhanging trees blocked the sun, and streams of water ran down the mountain and across the road.

"Hold on, everybody!" Sophie kept two hands on the steering wheel, gave out a short whoop, and stepped on the gas to go over the top of a hill.

Harry and Stella shouted in unison, "Whoa!" and the twins screamed happily as their stomachs jumped. Then they coasted down to the bottom.

Finally, a squeal of brakes, and Sophie made a sharp right switch-back turn onto a dirt path that ran parallel with River Road.

They bumped their way into the Fish Camp on the bank of the river, passing rough-hewn cabins along the way.

The five-foot circular sign, made from an old logger saw their Daddy had painted white, was standing at the entrance to the driveway of the family's Cabin, just as Stella remembered it. In big, dark blue letters, it read:

WELCOME TO FRED'S
Boats—Bait—Cabins

THREE

Opening Up

Stella's mother maneuvered the car as close as she could to the back porch of the Cabin. Before everyone started scrambling out, she stopped them.

"Okay, let's remember the rules." She pointed her finger at the twins in the back seat.

"Stosh and Elsie, you may NOT go down to the water alone. We don't want a repeat of last year when Stosh nearly drowned in the bait trough. Stay in the Cabin or with Stella until we get everything unpacked. Understood?" She looked sternly at the twins.

"Yes, Mama," they replied, their eyes downward. "We'll stay with Stella."

"Harry, can you turn the water on by yourself? I'll switch the electricity on first, and then you can start the pump. That's how you do it, right?"

"Yeah, Ma, I know what to do. Just let me know when you got the power on. Once we get the pump going, I'll go down the cellar and start a fire."

"Thank heaven I have you!" their mother leaned over Peppy and gave Harry a hug.

Within the hour, the Cabin was aglow with lights, they had running water, and trickle of heat was coming through the vents in the Cabin floor.

Stella and her mother took all the goose-down covers and pillows to the clothesline and shook the winter smell out of them. Together they unpacked the car and made up the beds. Harry carried several loads of firewood into the cellar and stacked them near the wood stove.

Stella and Harry lugged one of the 5 HP Evinrude outboard motors down to the dock to put on the No. 1 wooden boat. There was half a foot of water in the bright orange ten-foot scow, so Stella bailed it out with the faded "HILLS BROS" coffee can and wiped up the rest with an old towel.

When she finished, they lugged the motor onto the back of the dry boat. Harry lowered it into the water and secured the motor with clamps. Then he attached the safety chain.

Stella quickly cleaned up the second boat for tomorrow's fishermen. After Harry checked for oil and gas, he tried to start the motor. The engine turned over on the second try. He revved it for a while, then shut it off.

"They shouldn't have any problem, Stel. Sounds like it's running great."

Together they checked the dock lines for all six orange boats and walked up the steep, wooden steps leading from the dock to the top of the bank. The sun was just about to set, peep frogs were chirping, and the shadows were deep and dark.

They could hear the twins running around in the Cabin and saw warm light shining through the windows. Harry put his arm around his sister's shoulders.

"It sure feels good to be back here, doesn't it?" Stella felt she and Harry connected to the Cabin the best.

"Oh yes, I love it here. I hope I'll get to live here for the rest of my life!"

Harry turned to his sister. "You know, Stel, this is an important year for Dad and Ma. We really need to do a good business this summer, or the bank might take the Cabin." Harry stuffed his hands in his pockets.

"Dad got behind in payments this spring when the twins had to have their tonsils out, and the hospital bill was a heavy hit."

"I know. I overheard them talking about it the other day." Stella kicked a black walnut off the path.

"You know, Harry, in a way I think Mama wouldn't be all that upset to lose the Cabin, but I don't know if I could handle it." Stella's throat started that knot again and she shook her head and looked back out at the river.

"Well, let's just hope we have good weather for the July 4th weekend this year." Harry closed the barn doors of the cellar, and they went inside.

Supper smelled wonderful! Stella's mother cooked sauerkraut and Polish sausage to go with mashed potatoes and homemade pickled red beets. All that was missing was the tapioca pudding still sitting in the refrigerator back home.

* * *

"Okay, you guys," Stella said to the twins after dinner. "Are you ready to play Piggy?"

"Yeah, yeah!" Stosh and Elsie jumped up and knelt on chairs at the round oak table.

Stella spread a deck of cards face down on the table in a big circle. Then she randomly picked one card, turned it over, and put a Queen of Clubs face up in the middle of the pile.

"Okay, Elsie, you go first and try to find a club to match this card," Stella said.

Elsie picked up cards, making a disgusted face each time one wasn't a club.

"Finally," she said, and stuck her tongue out at Stosh who had hee-hawed and oinked every time Elsie ended up with one more piggy.

She put the club on the forming pile and then put a diamond on top of it. She smiled devilishly at Stosh and said, "Your turn. Try to find a diamond."

Stosh picked up cards until he found a matching diamond, but Elsie snickered after every card until he found it. Their turns continued until there weren't any more cards to uncover. Stosh still had three cards left.

"Ha, ha, Stosh. You have three piggies, oink, oink, oink." Elsie laughed until she nearly fell off her chair.

Stosh narrowed his eyes at Elsie. "I think YOU cheated."

Stella heard the argument from the kitchen where she was helping her mother. She hurried into the room and came over to the table. "Hey, you two are getting pretty good at this game." She complimented both twins to stop a brewing fight.

"You know your shapes and colors, for sure!" Piggy was definitely helping them learn to count, Stella thought. At this rate, they're both going to be pretty smart in school.

"Okay, you two, time for bed." Her mother had finished cleaning up the kitchen from supper and came over to the table covered with cards. "Tomorrow is a busy day." She herded the twins toward their bedroom.

"Stella," Stosh ran back to his sister, hugged her, and pleaded, "Will you take us to Peter Pan Rock tomorrow, please?" He exaggerated the "please" and stared up at Stella with his big brown eyes.

"Alright, if Mama says it's okay, you and Elsie and I will have a picnic on Peter Pan Rock. Now, get to bed."

After her mother tucked in the twins, Stella heard her talking on the phone and figured it was to her daddy.

"Well, we made out okay. We have water, power, and heat, thanks to Harry's help. And they got the boats ready too. What time will we see you tomorrow?"

Mama was quiet for a minute, then said, "Okay. See you then. Oh, don't forget to bring the tapioca pudding. Bye."

Stella heard rummaging in the kitchen. Her mother came into the living room carrying a tray with three steaming cups of hot chocolate and a dish of macaroon coconut cookies.

Stella and Harry were playing a card game called War. In this game the deck is shared, and the players each put a card face up at the same time. Whoever has the highest card wins both.

If both are the same value card, there is a War, and each player puts three more cards at risk face down. Then each player puts the next card face up, and whoever has the highest card wins all.

But today, Harry was holding all the luck. Stella could see her pile of cards dwindling away. She was happy to hear her mother enter the room.

"Well, Dad says he'll be here by four tomorrow. Do you two want to go out and sit on the porch awhile? Get coats or a blanket because it is getting cool out there!"

"Alright! I'll get my jacket. Stel, I won anyway; you have to admit it." Harry bounded out of the room.

"Sometimes he gets so lucky, Mama." Stella was gathering the cards from their game.

"Well, he is two years older than you. You will get better at it," her mother tried to reassure her.

"I'll go get a blanket off the bed to cover us." Stella went to the extra bedroom and got a warm feather comforter that is called a pierzyna in Polish to take to the back porch.

On the screened porch there was a glider at one end. All three sat there huddled, and their mother covered everyone with the feather pierzyna. It still smelled a little musty from the winter stay in the Cabin, but between it and the hot chocolate, everyone was toasty warm.

"Listen to the peep frogs, Harry." Stella sipped her warm drink. "They are in full chorus tonight!"

The night was crisp and cool. From the porch, Stella could see the full moon glistening on the surface of the river.

Occasionally a fish would jump, followed by a splash, and Stella would see the ripples vibrating on the water in the moonlight.

The sounds were those of early summer—peep frogs in gleeful chorus, and now and then an owl, very close, very loud.

Then a sharp, "Snap!" A branch broke in the nearby woods. Stella sat upright. "WHAT WAS THAT?"

"Oh, it's probably a raccoon, but maybe it's One Hand Sid coming to getcha!" Harry reached over his mother and grabbed Stella's arm. She jumped up and ran to latch the screen door on the porch.

"Do you really believe that story about One Hand Sid, Harry? How did he lose his hand?"

"He pulled off a robbery at one of the Catskill resorts, but got away, and they never found the jewelry he stole. I heard he cut off his own hand to get away."

"Sounds to me like hokum," Stella said, not believing him.

"Oh no, Stel. They got the proof. Dad said the police found his hand and froze it so when they catch him, they'll be able to compare fingerprints. He was a bigtime gangster, I'll tell ya."

Harry rocked back in the glider. "And they think he's probably still hiding out somewhere in these mountains."

Their mother finally had enough of the "One Hand Sid" story.

Exasperated, she said, "Look, you two, we don't need that kind of talk out here in the middle of nowhere, and in the dark, so think of something else to talk about, okay?" Their mother crossed her arms against her chest and sighed.

Stella laughed and took in a deep breath. "Mama, just smell that fresh air. I'll bet those people in Coalville wish they were here."

The air was a mix of wet forest, overgrown grass, and the river.

To Stella, these were the best of times! Cuddled on either side of their mother, she and Harry remembered past summers at the Cabin and what this summer might hold in store.

They laughed about the greenie fishermen that came to rent boats, and didn't even know how to row, and kept going in circles in front of the dock until her mother or Harry yelled instructions to them.

Stella was always amazed that grown men couldn't figure out how to start a motor or change a shear pin after they hit a rock.

And they laughed all over again when Harry reminded them about the time Mr. Feeney, in his striped city pants and wingtip shoes, was trying to impress his new girlfriend and, while getting into the boat, fell backwards into the water.

"I remember that was a pretty funny sight Harry, but Mama, tell us the Drowned Baby Story again," Stella begged.

"Oh Stella," you know how I hate to even remember that night." She twisted her hands together and held them close to her chest.

Reluctantly, her mother retold the story about the time her daddy convinced her mother to go out on the water one night to gig eels, and by the light of the Coleman lantern attached to the front of the boat, her mother saw a baby, lying face up and drowned, on the pebbly bottom of the river.

"I screamed so loud I know they heard me in New York City!" Their mother cradled her face in her hands and continued.

"Daddy caught the baby's dress with the gig, but when he brought it to the surface, it was only a baby doll."

Later they laughed about it, but their mother said she could never forget her feeling of horror at seeing what she thought was a dead baby in the water.

Their mother looked at her watch. It was after ten, and they would need to be up at five-thirty to be ready for the fishermen.

"Ok, kids, let's call it a night. Harry, did you get Mr. Ward's bait ready for him?"

"I sure did! I put a dozen nice-size lamprey eels in a pail with sand and water. I have them ready at the bottom of the steps at the trapdoor. Is Dad still going to charge a dollar per dozen this year?"

"No, he told me we need to charge $1.50 per dozen, except for a few certain customers. But he thought Mr. Ward could afford the higher price."

Their mother turned and looked at Stella and Harry. In a concerned voice, she said, "I know both of you are too young to worry about money issues, but you've always helped Dad and me so much in this business, I'm sure you understand how much it helps the family. Let's just hope we can make enough money this summer so we can pay some important bills, and maybe Dad can borrow enough for a new panel truck. I'm really worried one of these days that old engine's just going to give out."

Stella and Harry kept secret their knowledge of the "important bills" and just looked at each other. Their mother hugged them both and said, "You and Stella did a wonderful job getting everything ready. I couldn't have done it without you. Now you better go to bed and get some sleep."

Stella hugged her mother back and said, "Don't worry, Mama, we have a feeling this is going to be a great summer."

She hugged them both again, and they went off to bed.

Stella listened as her mother locked up all the doors, shut off the lights, and shuffled to her own bed.

She heard the mattress squeak and then a deep sigh. She knew Mama wasn't very happy to be back up the Cabin.

FOUR

Weekend Fishermen

Stella was dreaming about her horse, the one she'd own after she sold one thousand tins of Cloverine salve. This opportunity was advertised on the back cover of certain comic books, and it had a picture of a Palomino pony with a beautiful saddle and bridle. She was going to send away for the information this summer and she was sure she could sell this salve to all the fishermen.

In her dream, she was brushing her horse's sleek, golden neck with long smooth strokes while the horse was munching on sweet new hay.

The rhythmic sound of the horse chewing hay somehow turned into a low murmur of voices, and Stella left her dream world, waking up in her bed at the Cabin.

The voices were those of her mother and Harry. The windup clock by her bed showed a quarter to six, and the faint glow of sunrise was sneaking through the slits in the blinds.

Harry and her mother were already up and dressed, so Stella threw on the same clothes she had worn yesterday and went into the kitchen.

Mm. Stella inhaled the smell of fresh coffee. She had only started drinking coffee this year, and she loved it with lots of sugar and milk.

Harry had gone down to the cellar through the trapdoor to add a few pieces of wood to the fire. Even though it was the middle of June, nights on the river were chilly.

"Harry, don't forget to bring up Mr. Ward's bait," his mother reminded him in a hushed tone through the trapdoor. She did not want to wake up the twins.

Just as Harry climbed up through the hole with the can of bait in his hand, there was knocking on the back porch door.

"Good, just in time. One thing is for sure, Mr. Ward always likes an early start," she said.

She went onto the back porch and unlatched the screen door. "Good morning, Ed. Looks like you will have a pretty day for fishing. I just made a pot of coffee. Would you men like some while you're getting your gear together? Harry's got your bait ready."

The fisherman smiled at her through the screened door. "Sophie, that would be great. We left Tamaqua about four, made good time, but didn't stop for coffee. How much do we owe you for the boats, bait, and cabin this year?"

Stella's mother opened the screen door and went out. "The cabin's still ten dollars per night on the weekend, and the boat and motor are still three dollars per day with the extra boat at a dollar-fifty, just like last year."

Then Stella's mother took a deep breath and said, "Fred said the lamprey eels are going up to a dollar-fifty a dozen because they are getting harder to find. I guess with all the building going on, some of his favorite spots for digging are gone. I'll go pour some coffee and bring it out."

Sophie paused for a moment to see Mr. Ward's reaction to the price increase of the lampreys, but he just kept smiling at her. As she turned to go back into the Cabin, Harry came out with the can of bait. He tilted it toward Mr. Ward.

"Look, I gave you some pretty big ones," Harry said.

The two-pound coffee can had about three inches of sand in the bottom and the same amount of water above it. Harry dug his hand into the sand, and small lamprey eels, called elvers, started swimming around in the water.

"You've got about a half dozen that are at least five inches, and others about half that size. My dad and I dug these two weekends ago near Hancock Creek." Harry took his hand out of the chilly water, wiped it on his jeans, and handed the can to Mr. Ward.

"Good luck with them. Don't forget to hook the eel as close to the tail as possible. That way they'll last longer and be more active in the water. My dad said they're catching nice bass down by the bridge, but stay on the left-hand side, in the eddy."

Harry, remembering what his dad had told him, looked down, shuffled his feet, and said, "Mr. Ward, remind everybody once they go past the bridge, the current gets pretty strong, and if they aren't careful, they'll end up in those rapids down there."

He looked up at Mr. Ward, forcing a smile. "If you hit a rock and break the shear pin, you're going to be in trouble."

"Thanks, Harry, I will remind them. I only needed it to happen to me one time." He took the can and headed toward his car and fishing friends.

Stella, Harry, and their mother took out mugs of hot coffee on trays along with a stack of thick-sliced, buttered rye bread. They put these on the picnic table. All four men gathered round.

Stella noted they came in a new, shiny red car. She glanced at Harry to see his reaction. She saw him drop his jaw and shake his head in disbelief.

Mr. Ward walked over to Stella. "And how's my favorite fishing guide?" He gave her a hug. Then he pulled a wad of bills from his back pocket and peeled off a few, handing them to Stella's mother.

"Thanks for taking care of us, Sophie." He smiled what seemed to Stella to be an extra warm smile, and when her mother reached for the money, he held it for just an extra moment. She grabbed the bills, shoved them into her apron pocket, and waved them a great day.

"Fred said you wanted Cabin Two for tonight. We'll have it ready when you get off the water," she said and backed away, taking Stella with her.

As they walked to the Cabin, Stella could hear the fishermen making bets on who would catch the biggest, or most fish, and deciding what the payout would be for the winner.

Mr. Ward had been coming to the Fish Camp for as long as Stella could remember, and Fred considered him to be one of their best customers. The car he came in this year was a brand-new, 1955 red Cadillac. Her father always said Mr. Ward had money, but now Stella knew for sure. *Wait until Daddy sees this car!*

Once inside the Cabin, Stella got right in Harry's face with white showing all around her eyeballs. "DO YOU SEE THAT CAR!" she said. "I can't imagine how much THAT cost!"

Harry pushed his sister's face away from him. "Yeah, I saw it when I first went out to give him the bait. I tried to keep my jaw from falling off my face. Figured I would wait until they got on the river before going over to take a good look at it. Man, that guy must be rich."

"Oh yeah, I suspect he is," their mother clucked. "He's a good customer," then as an afterthought said, "but a flirt too. Although I don't think he means anything by it."

She paused for a thoughtful moment and then said, "Come on, let's have a nice breakfast and get this day going."

* * *

Stella was helping her mother clean up Cabin 2 for Mr. Ward and his fishing buddies. They were putting clean sheets on one of the wrought-iron beds.

"Mama, when are the Barconis coming for the summer?"

"I think Sal told Daddy it would be sometime this week. Their schools don't get out for a few more days." The Barconi girls were Stella's best friends in the Fish Camp.

"And are those neat folks from Brooklyn coming back this year? You know, the family with the girls Deana and Betty?"

"Oh, the Shirota's? Yes, they are here for July 4th week, and I think they're coming back the last week in August too," her mother replied.

After they finished cleaning the cabin for the fishermen, her mother told Stella it would be okay to take the twins swimming. "But stay by the dock, Stella. Those two cannot swim as well as you."

"I'll watch them. Oh Mama, don't forget last year you promised me this year you would let me swim across the whole river, right?"

"Oh, you never forget anything, do you?" her mother used her exasperated voice. "I promised, but you have to do it when Harry can row the boat next to you in case you get tired, okay?"

"Okay. Mama, how come you don't ever swim?"

"I just never learned how," she replied. "Daddy tried to teach me a couple of times, but I just get too nervous. I really don't even like the water. But you kids got his swimming talent for sure because you and Harry swim like fish."

* * *

In early June, the river was pretty cold. Stella jumped off the edge of the dock, but she was still only waist deep in the cool clear water.

"Now wait here 'til I get all wet." She motioned to the twins to sit at the edge of the dock, took a deep breath, and dove in.

"WOW," she told the twins after she surfaced, rubbing her arms to get her circulation going again. "I hope the river warms up soon." Then she helped each of them jump into the water.

"Yeehaw, it's COLD!" screamed Elsie.

"Don't worry, you'll get used to it," Stella comforted her. "In a few minutes, it'll feel warm; wait and see."

In their new Minnie Mouse and Pluto inner tubes, the twins splashed at the edge of the dock, and Stella checked out the pebbly bottom of the river.

She stuck her face into the crystal-clear water and looked around at the rocky bottom. She spied a god stone, a flat white pebble, scooped it up and rubbed it clean. Minnows nibbled at her toes and flashed their shiny sides. Soon, larger blue gills and sunfish arrived to investigate, but stayed at a distance.

"Look, my first god stone!" Stella showed the twins her finding and let them admire it.

"Why do they call it a god stone?" Stosh asked.

Stella knew this was coming. She looked around them, at the mountains bordering the clear river, white clouds in a bright blue sky above, and said, "I guess because it lives in God's country."

Then she took the pebble from her brother, bent her knees, and skipped it across the surface of the water. One, two, three skips and it settled back onto the river's bottom.

FIVE

Misty

"Stella, you are in charge in case any fishermen come while we are gone! Give them No. 3 boat if they want one and go through the trapdoor in the house to get bait. Remember do not let anyone in the cellar or in the Cabin. We won't be gone long." After her lecture to Stella, her mother headed to the car.

Her mother, Harry, and the twins piled in and soon were chugging up the hill from the Fish Camp to drive the mile of winding river road and cross the Darbytown Bridge to town for groceries.

Stella stood in the dirt driveway and watched as the car turned left onto the paved River Road. As they passed above the Cabin, her mother honked the horn twice, and Stella heard the twins yelling, "Bye, Stella!"

Stella walked to the swing by the firepit that overlooked the river and plopped herself in the middle. The ancient black walnut tree shaded the swing, and the cabins stood behind her. Her feet spragged the dirt each time she swung back, and the swing squeaked a rhythm to a song in Stella's head.

"Somewhere, over the rainbow, way up high," then another sound entered the song. Stella heard a distant, rhythmic clip-clop of horse hooves on the paved road above the Cabin. It wasn't Mr. Gannett's team of workhorses, Tom and Ginny. This was the sound of one set of hooves, and she

33

knew the rider was probably the redheaded girl on the beautiful white horse she had seen riding along River Road last fall.

The clippity-clop was closer now, and Stella knew by the sound, the white horse would soon appear on the road above the Cabin. This time she would take the chance and try to meet them at the top of the road before they passed. Her plan was if she made it in time, she'd pretend she was just checking the mailbox.

Stella caught a glimpse of white above her and started to run. She took a shortcut between two of the rental cabins and jumped the small stream fed from the spring coming out of the mountainside. She landed at the edge of the stream, and the cool water soaked one of her sneakers and it sloshed as she ran up the hill.

The rhythm of the beating hooves changed, and she recognized by the new pattern the horse was in a rapid trot. Stella ran as fast as she could up the clay path, but as she reached the top of the road, she saw a white tail waving at her and the back of a red-haired rider posting effortlessly on her horse. River Road was straight and wide in this stretch. It was a good place to trot safely.

But Stella was disappointed. Pouting, she kicked a black walnut off the edge of the road into the ditch and shuffled to the top, her chin resting on her chest. She watched as the horse slowed to a walk, turned by Peter Pan's Rock, and disappeared into the road. She stood there until the echo of hooves mingled with the sounds of the forest.

She dejectedly walked to the silver mailbox and opened it with a snap. Nothing! Mama must have checked it before she went into town. She was hoping for a letter from Helen.

Stella, now even more depressed, shuffled back down the dirt road to the cabins. Halfway down the hill, she stopped at Big Rock. When the land was cleared for the cabins, Big Rock was saved. The men were going to dynamite it into small pieces, but the children begged to leave it.

It was flat and fairly smooth on the surface, about two feet high at the base, and was the favorite meeting place for all the kids in the Fish Camp. The other end rose from the ground and at the top was easily six feet high. It could hold all twenty children in the camp.

There were many cracks and crevices along the sides of the rock where the children often hid treasures, rabbit tobacco, and notes. This was the home base for hide and seek and the site of truce after major battles.

A freshwater spring ran through a pipe under the dirt road and snaked its way along the side of Big Rock and down towards the river. Mayapple plants sprouted from the moist ground on the sides of the stream.

Stella looked around for a mayapple plant with ripe fruit. She and her friends called them Umbrella plants because the leaves spread out from the top of the foot-high plant like an umbrella. The fruit, when ripe, was the pale-yellow color of honey. The children had all been warned that green unripe mayapples were poisonous, and Stella had to make sure the twins didn't eat them.

Stella picked the ripest ones she could find, climbed onto Big Rock, and carefully made her way to the highest point. From here she could see the river, all the way from the top of the rapids to the bend in the eddy.

Stella squeezed the base of the mayapple until the top popped open and sweet juicy pulp with tiny seeds oozed out. She sucked the amber juice and savored the tropical flavor.

Then she lay back and enjoyed the warmth radiating from the gray rock, focused on a certain white cloud moving quickly by, and thought about a plan of how to meet the girl with the white horse.

* * *

When Stella's father got to the Cabin that weekend, Stella had her plan ready. After dinner Saturday night, she sat next to him on the couch while he was reading the newspaper.

"Daddy, I have a question," she started.

He put down the paper and looked at her, "And that question is?"

"Well, you know the barn where the girl keeps her white horse down on River Road. Where the pasture goes down to the creek?" She had a habit of twirling a strand of hair at the back of her head when she was nervous.

"Yeah, I know where you mean. Where are you going with this, Stel?" He peered down at her with his dark eyes showing above the edge of his glasses.

"Well, doesn't that barn belong to Mr. Gannett where he keeps his extra hay and equipment?"

"Yeah, that's Mr. Gannett's property and barn. So?"

"Well," now Stella was really twirling her hair and started talking more quickly. "I wondered if you could ask Mr. Gannett the name of the girl that owns the white horse so I could call her and see if she would let me meet her at the barn sometime." Stella stopped twirling and sat quietly with her head down and hands between her knees, waiting.

Her father chuckled and said, "I could do that before I leave for town. I am supposed to call Mr. Gannett tomorrow about a canoe he has for sale. I'll ask him then, okay?"

Stella's head shot up, "Oh yes, Daddy, thanks a lot!" She hugged her father's neck and ran off to find someone to tell.

* * *

Stella hung the receiver back into its cradle. She was really nice to invite me to the barn to meet her and Misty, Stella thought.

Her name was Suzanna, and she lived in town with her parents and a brother named Brad. They had moved here last fall from upstate New York. She said they felt lucky to find a nice barn like Mr. Gannett's to keep Misty. Suzanna's father had just bought another horse, an old mare named Sully to keep Misty Company, and Suzanna asked if Stella would like to ride with her sometime.

Inside, Stella was shouting, Yes, Yes, Yes! But as calmly as she could, she said, "Oh that would be great!" They agreed to meet at the barn on Monday morning at nine.

Her mother gave Stella a lecture on horses, the size of horses, the danger of horses, and every terrible thing her mother ever heard about horses. Then her mother gave her a hug and told her to have fun and to be careful.

Stella left for her mile walk to the barn with plenty of spare time, but when she got there, Suzanna already had Misty cross-tied between two poles and was brushing him. She stopped when she saw Stella walking down the dirt path from River Road, gave Misty a reassuring pat, and walked up to the gate to meet her.

"Hi, you must be Stella," Suzanna stuck her hand out. Stella shook it more than she needed. "My mom dropped me off at the barn a little early so she could do some errands so I thought I could start cleaning up the horses."

"I saw you and Misty on River Road a few times last year but never got the chance to catch up with you. Misty has a fast trot!"

"Oh yeah, he loves to trot. It is his favorite gait, and it's pretty comfortable when you post. Do you know how?"

Stella knew this moment would come, but she had to face it. *The sooner the better.*

"You know, Suzanna, I've read a hundred books about horses, but other than a pony our daddy bought for my brother Harry a couple of summers ago, I've never had riding lessons. Do you think I can learn quickly?"

Suzanna let out a laugh and flung her bright red hair out of her eyes. She opened the gate for Stella and shut it after she walked into the pasture.

"Don't worry, Stella. I'll have you posting in no time. But I must tell you, it's not as easy on Sully. She's about twenty-six years old, which is over a hundred in people years. When my dad bought her, they told him that a long time ago she got into a barrel of sweet feed and foundered, which left her with a limp, so her gait isn't as smooth as Misty's. But she will be easier to ride because she isn't as headstrong as this white monster."

When they walked over to Misty, Suzanna tickled his pink velvet nose. The horse squiggled his upper lip, almost like a smile.

Suzanna added as an afterthought, "Oh, and if it should happen, it's not as far to fall." She grimaced at Stella and shrugged her shoulders matter-of-factly.

Over the summer, Suzanna taught Stella how to curry comb and brush Sully and Misty before a ride and to scrape and rinse off their sweat afterwards. The horses liked grooming.

She learned to saddle and bridle, clean hooves, and braid manes and tails. But the real fun came when they mounted and rode across the fields in the early morning dew and in the late afternoons when the sun was setting.

One afternoon, a thunderstorm caught the girls by surprise when they were about a mile from the barn. They dismounted, grabbed up the reins, and stood under the trees at the edge of a field, getting soaked and laughing about their predicament.

That's when Stella learned to count the seconds after a lightning strike, to hear the thunder and calculate how far away the lightning really was. One-elephant, two-elephant; five elephants meant the lightning was one mile away.

When the rain stopped, they remounted their horses and headed back to the barn.

SIX

The Fire!

Harry and Stella, twins in tow, walked up the dirt path to the top of River Road and headed left toward town. They figured to get as far as the Darbytown Bridge before they met their father's truck. If he wasn't there by then, they could sit on the guardrail and keep watch, since there was no other road he might take. It was late Saturday afternoon, and as usual, Fred came from town to spend the night and would have to leave Sunday evening to go back to work.

"Come on, you guys! Put some oomph into your feet, or we won't even make the top of the hill before we meet him," Harry prodded the group along. They picked up the pace and jogged along the road above the Cabin.

Where River Road overlooked the Cabin, the twins yelled down to their mother together, "Hi Mama!"

She waved, and Peppy barked from inside the back porch. Mama said he would be safer with her than on the road.

Stella spied a patch of wild strawberries along the edge of the road and quickly picked a handful for the twins. Stosh stuffed a few in his mouth and squeezed the dark red juice through his teeth and smiled. Elsie ate hers one at a time. "Yipes, that one wasn't ripe!" and scrunched her face.

"Harry, I need a rest," Elsie whined, as they reached the spot above Barconi's cabin.

"Okay, it's time for a drink anyway."

A clear stream of spring water dripped from the mossy mountain ledge on the far side of the road. Harry put his mouth under the stream and caught a drink. Then everyone else took turns. Stosh got his hair wet, and Elsie let the water run down the front of her jumpsuit.

"Oh, you guys! I hope you dry off before Mama sees you, or I'm in trouble!" Stella fanned the front of Elsie's jumpsuit and tussled Stosh's hair to dry it.

Panting, they struggled up the last hill to the top. "Stella, I'm tired."

Stosh crawled over to a rock jutting out of the mountainside and sat down. He looked up beyond the tall pines to the ledges and caves above. "Is this where the poor people from the city come to live in the summer?"

"Yeah, this is the spot." One time, Stella, Harry, and their friends hiked up the mountainside and found bare mattresses underneath the rocky ledge, along with campfire coals, and lots of trash.

"Mama says these people come by train from the city and stay in the caves a good part of the summer. She doesn't even think they can speak English."

Once over the hill, walking was easier. Harry ran ahead, but Stella and the twins held hands and skipped down the small hill. At the bottom, Elsie pointed to the dirt road on the right.

"That's the way to Spooky Road; right, Stella?" Stella nodded; glad they were not going there now. In a few minutes they were at the Darbytown Bridge that crossed the river. Her mother gave definite orders not to go any further. The main road had too much traffic.

"We made it!" Stella told the twins. "Now keep an eye out for Daddy's truck."

They had just set up their post on the guardrail like a family of birds perched on a wire, when Harry yelled, "Here he comes! That's his blue truck for sure!"

A light-blue panel truck came down the main road. The brakes squeaked as it reached the bridge and then turned, and the driver tooted the horn and slowed alongside the group.

Harry shouted, "Hi there! Do you take hitchhikers?"

Daddy looked out the window, smiled, shook his head, and said, "If your last name is Karvotsky, come on board!"

Everybody laughed, and Stella sat the twins inside the front cab. Harry and Stella stood outside on the running boards. Daddy went slow, but when he drove over the top of the big hill, Stella's feet left the running board for a few seconds.

"WOW!" She screamed but held on tight. Harry was talking to Daddy through the driver's window, giving him updates on who came to fish and rent boats, and how much bait was sold.

When they got to the Cabin, Sophie and Peppy came to greet them, and Sophie got a big hug from Fred.

"Hi, Honeybuns! You had a good week without me?" He squeezed her waist and twirled her once full circle.

"Fred, Fred, let me go!" she laughed as her feet left the ground, and she was temporarily airborne. Then he gently released and held her so she wouldn't fall.

"Me next! I want to ride too!" After the twins got their airplane rides, they all headed for the Cabin.

"Fred, I have your favorite supper! Fresh corn on the cob, steak from the local butcher, simmered in light brown gravy with onions, and creamy mashed potatoes."

"Well, I brought a few Mama Mia sodas and a Dutch Apple pie. Sounds like we are going to have another feast!"

It always felt special on Saturday night when their father was with them, and he was usually in a good mood, happy to be at his favorite place in this world, with his family.

The twins were just finishing their apple pie when Harry piped up, "Dad, you aren't going to believe this story about the fishermen that came yesterday." he said.

"They were really dressed to the nines, with starched shirts and those shoes with the tassels on them." Harry rocked back in his chair.

"I asked them if they needed any help with the boat, but no, no, everything was fine. So, I shove them off at the dock and go up the bank, and we sit on the swing and watch them. For almost half an hour they row in circles in front of the dock."

Stella had to add to the story, "Harry and I were practically rolling on the ground."

This put everyone at the table in a fit of laughter. Harry calmed them down and continued, "Finally, I decided to go down and help them out. You would have been proud of me, I gave them rowing lessons, and in about fifteen minutes they were splashing away down the river. Of course, I ended up having to tow them back. Bet they slept well last night, though!"

Everybody laughed, and their father said, "You know, we are having a rather good season already. The cabins are full for July 4th. If we keep the boats rented, Ma and I are going to be able to pick out a new truck soon!"

They were having such a fun time, with everyone laughing and feeling good about the business when Stella remembered her mother always said, "Laugh today, cry tomorrow." That certainly came true that weekend.

* * *

Stella was shocked from a sound sleep by banging on the back-porch door. In a chain reaction the knocking set off Peppy barking and the twins crying. Her father ran down the hall and tripped over Peppy. The dog ran into the living room yelping. Her father finally reached the door to see who was banging and screaming like a banshee!

"Better not be some crazy fishermen!" he growled.

Stella's windup clock with the glowing face said three-fifteen. No way it could be fishermen, she thought.

"Who's there?" Fred called through the back door.

"Fred, Fred, it's me, Sal Barconi! We got trouble, BIG trouble. Joe Gannett's barn is on fire! They called from the Fire Station and asked me to pull together as much help as we could. I'm going over to Jim and Pete's and round up as many hands as we can from our camp. I'll come back in about ten minutes to get you and Harry, okay?"

"Sure, Sal. I'll get Harry, and we'll meet you out here." As her father turned, Harry, who heard the whole story, was already running back to his bedroom, pulling on his pants, grabbing a shirt, shoes, and jacket.

"Daddy, can I come? I can help; please let me come with you!" Stella was following him back to the bedroom, her hands clasped together, pleading.

Her father turned and looked sternly at Stella. "Stel, you need to stay here and help Ma with the twins." Then he hugged her mother and said, "Sophie, you think you could pull together coffee and sandwiches and bring it over to Gannett's? I'm sure Arlene will help too." He walked into the bedroom. "Let me get dressed."

It seemed like only minutes when Sal and the others honked the horn. "Dad, they're here. You ready?" Harry went to the back door.

"I'm right behind you, son." Harry and his dad left the porch and hopped into the back of the pickup.

Stella was trying to calm the twins, singing "this ole man, he played one," and all three were rocking together in Grama's big oak rocker.

Her mother brought out the extra big coffeepot and got it perking on the stove, then checked the pantry and refrigerator for sandwich makings. There was half a Polish apple cake in the freezer, and she took it out to thaw.

What about Tom and Ginny? Stella worried to herself over and over as she rocked, *Oh God, please let them be okay.* She had read many horse stories where, in a fire, the horses would not leave their stalls, no matter what the owners did to try to save them.

It was almost four a.m. before her mother and Arlene Barconi had all the food in the car. Her daughters Mannie and Lola helped.

"Mama, please let me and Mannie go with you, please. Lola agreed to babysit the twins."

Her mother turned and looked at Stella. She must have looked pathetic because she finally agreed.

As soon as her mother turned off River Road onto the main highway, Stella sniffed the air. "Oh, I smell something burning, Mama! You think it's the barn this far away?"

She didn't wait for an answer and said, "Mannie, look in the sky there. It's blood red! It must be the barn." The distant horizon had a reddish cast.

As soon as they arrived at the bottom of the hill below the barn, they could see the actual flames shooting out of it. There were two fire trucks spraying water and several dozen men circling at a distance, trying wherever possible to pull away a piece of farm equipment or some tack. Stella scanned the area. *Where are Tom and Ginny?*

Sophie parked the car a good distance away, and the girls piled out and walked as close as they could. Even at a distance of a few hundred feet, the heat from the fire was too much to stand. One fire truck backed further away because the paint started to blister.

Her mother spied Mrs. Gannett, wiping away tears with her apron, and ran up to her, taking hold of her by the shoulders. "Grace, I am so sorry. Is Joe okay? Are the animals safe?"

"Oh Sophie, we cannot believe this! Joe ran into the barn in stocking feet. I know he's burnt them bad. He got the heifer and the goats out, but, but Tom and Ginny. . ."

Grace Gannett sobbed in Sophie's arms like a mother that has lost her children. Then Stella knew, those two beautiful creatures she had stroked so many times, that loved each other as if they were human, and were so loved by their owners and friends, were gone. She walked behind a laurel bush and cried; she hoped the heaven Sister Gerry talked about in school also took in horses.

It was well into the morning before the flames were under control. The firemen gathered their equipment, coiled dirty wet hoses, and folded ladders. The rescue team had drunk huge pots of coffee and stacks of sandwiches that Sophie and Arlene served.

Sergeant McFaddy, the Fire Chief, approached the group of women from the Fish Camp. "Ladies, we thank ya for your help, both moral support and food. We just wish it could have turned out different." He turned, his head down, and walked back to help his men.

The heat from the fire was more isolated now. Stella broke away from the women and was able to actually walk close to the remains of the barn. She tried to find the spot where Tom and Ginny shared their stall.

Daddy gripped her shoulders from behind. "Stel, I know how much those horses meant to you. I am sorry for all of us." He wrapped his arms around her, and together they walked as close as possible to Tom and Ginny's stall.

There, in one corner, were two humps of burned remains, one slightly smaller than the other. You could easily make out the smaller hump rested against the larger one.

Stella thought about their first trip to the Cabin next summer, and what it would be without the game of who would see Mr. Gannett's red barn first. The fire took away not only two incredibly special animals, Tom and Ginny, but also a very special part of her childhood.

SEVEN

Daddy's On Vacation!

The Fourth of July weekend was always the busiest time at the Fish Camp. Stella's father's bakery closed for the whole week, so he took a vacation from delivering bread and got to spend it with the family at the Cabin.

July 4th was on a Monday this year, so her father got to the Cabin early on Saturday afternoon. Since Tom and Ginny had died in the fire, he promised to take Stella, Harry, and their friends for a hayride in a makeshift trailer. It would never be the same as being pulled in a wagon by those beautiful horses, but he was determined they would have a hayride. However, as usual with her father, there was a condition.

"Okay, Stel," he told her as they walked together toward the truck. "We'll do the hayride, but remember part of the deal is you guys pick night crawlers once we're at the golf course on top of Shiflin Mountain, right?"

Daddy always got a little work out of every deal he made with the family.

He backed his panel truck to the hitch of a rusty red trailer, which was really the bed of an old pickup with wooden slats attached on all three sides. He hitched it to the truck and put on two safety chains.

Mr. Gannett had donated a freshly cut bale of green alfalfa hay from the barn where Misty stayed. Her father cut the twine bands with his ivory-covered pocketknife, and together he and Stella spread it on the trailer floor. He jumped out while Stella spread the last of it.

Stella jumped down before her father slammed the tailgate shut. "You're still going to pay a penny a piece for the nightcrawlers we catch, right?" she asked.

"I know Lola and Mannie need some spending money, and Harry said Lester and the other guys want the extra cash too!"

"Oh yes! That is the deal, and we need at least five hundred crawlers to get us through July 4th and the rest of the season. I might even have to buy some more toward end of August from that weasel down in Cohocton."

Her father leaned against the trailer. "It rained last night, so we should have good pickings on the greens. Tell the gang to be ready at eight tonight and bring flashlights with good batteries. We'll make up enough cans, so everybody has their own."

He tugged at the safety chains one more time. "Well, the trailer's ready. Let's get those bait cans ready."

Stella followed her father to the cellar. When he swung open the heavy wooden doors, Stella felt a rush of musty cool air. He tromped down the steps with Stella close behind. The cans were in the back room, where she hated to go by herself.

But with her father here, she didn't mind. He had wired the whole cellar with lights, and he turned them on, one at a time, as they maneuvered through the small bait rooms and into the back.

Along the wall facing the mountain, a wooden ladder led to a trapdoor into the kitchen above. This is how Harry got the bait for fishermen when they came at night or early in the morning.

A woodstove that stood on one side had a smokestack and two pieces of silver tubing, which looked like arms extending up in the air and ended at vents in the floor above. Her father had designed the heating system himself.

He rummaged around in a dark corner and came back into the light with two armfuls of five-pound steel vegetable cans, some with their wrappers still on. Each had a loop of wire across the top to make a handle. He dumped these on the floor and then dragged out a burlap bag full of moss from the same corner.

"Here, Stel, put some of this moss in each of the cans, and then we will wet them down a little. Don't put in too much, just enough to cover the bottom. We don't want the worms to crawl out after all the work it takes to get them in there."

Stella dug into the bag of moss, pulled out a handful of the foamy green stuff, separated it a bunch at a time, and laid it into the cans. She thought about how many people were going to pick night crawlers and counted Stella, Lola, Mannie, Harry, Lester, Joey, and Chi-Chi. There was one extra. She guessed her father planned to pick, too. When she handed the cans to him, he sprayed each one with the hose for a few seconds.

"That does it. Let's put these in the truck and see what Ma has for supper tonight." Stella stayed close behind, shut off lights as they left each room, followed him up the cellar steps, and slammed the cellar doors shut. Together they put the cans in the back of the truck.

When Stella opened the Cabin door, she savored the smell of sauerkraut and steamed cabbage. She knew what her mother had cooked for supper—golumbki and sauerkraut! The filling of the golumbki was steamed rice mixed with onions, tomato sauce, ground beef and pork. Her mother always added extra parsley and seasoned breadcrumbs.

In the kitchen her mother was taking the last batch of potato pancakes out of the black iron skillet.

"Here, wash your hands and put these on the table." Sophie handed Stella a huge platter of crispy brown pancakes. Harry had just finished setting the table.

Stella gathered up the twins and helped them settle in their seats. She took her spot between Stosh and Harry.

"Harry," Stella started. "Daddy said everybody picking night crawlers needs to be ready at eight with their own flashlights. After dinner I'll tell Lola and Mannie. Want me to stop by Zulach's and tell the guys?"

"Sure, all of us guys are sleeping in the tent tonight so they're probably there. Are the bait cans ready?"

Stella frowned at her brother. "Duh! Daddy and I got them ready. And we put the hay in the trailer, too."

"Oh, that's why I had to do your dirty work setting the table, huh! So, how many crawlers are you going to pick?"

Stella thought a minute. "Daddy says he needs a couple hundred. Maybe I'll try for a hundred. How about you?"

Fred and Sophie walked into the room and settled themselves at the table. Sophie challenged Harry, "So how many worms are you agreeing to catch tonight?"

Harry stabbed two potato pancakes and put them on his plate, then smothered them with his mother's warm homemade applesauce. "Well, Ma, depends on how long we're out there. If we start picking at nine, I guess the girls will be ready to go home in a couple of hours, so I might get a couple hundred or so. Here, Stella, you want the applesauce?"

"No, I'm having sour cream on mine." Stella spooned a hefty topping of white cream on her pancakes and smoothed it evenly over the top of each one. "Okay, Harry, I'll make a bet with you. Whoever gets the least crawlers does the dinner dishes for a week. Deal?"

"Deal!" Harry mumbled; his mouth was full of golumbki.

"Ahh, a bit of competition tonight I see," their father just chuckled.

After supper, Stella and Harry cleaned up, while her mother put away leftovers and helped the twins. When Harry fed Peppy, he even poured some golumbki juice on his dry food.

Peppy gobbled it up so fast Harry said, "Wow, hope we don't see that again too soon, like all over the floor."

Stella saw what he did, shook her head, and said, "Better let him stay on the porch while we're gone tonight. It will be easier to clean up there."

Stella peeked into the living room where her dad was spread out on the couch, taking his usual after-dinner nap, listening to evening news on the old-timey standup radio.

Stella wished they had a television at the Cabin.

Last winter, her parents had bought a black and-white TV as the whole family's main Christmas present. The shiny brown wooden cabinet had a big screen in the middle and speakers on the bottom. Her mother put the statue of the Blessed Mother on top of it. Getting that TV was exciting because only a few of Stella's friends had one.

The Philco dealer had a special promotion as a part of the purchase, and Stella's family got two cases of Mama Mia's homemade soda each week for eight weeks. Her mother always ordered the flavors mixed, and when they were delivered, she had them put in the canning cellar to stay cold. The soda was in clear, bumpy glass bottles, and because the flavors were mixed, it looked like a case of rainbow colors—orange, lime green, grape, and cherry.

As a special treat when watching TV, her mother would cook up a batch of popcorn in the wire-basket popper on top of the gas stove. Then she would drizzle melted butter over it until it puddled in the bottom of the bowl. Everybody got their own flavor of soda; Stella loved golden cream best.

She already had some favorite TV shows like "I Love Lucy." Her father did not really seem all that excited about TV. He'd watch news and The Ed Sullivan Show on Sunday night, but since he had to get up by four-thirty every morning, he couldn't stay up longer than nine. That's when Dragnet came on, which Stella, Harry and their mother watched every week. It was an exciting show with lots of shooting.

Sometimes Daddy would even yell down from the upstairs bedroom, "Turn that thing down!" That made Stella feel bad, as if her father were missing being part of the family.

But Stella loved being at the Cabin so much, giving up TV to be there wasn't a big deal. She left her father napping on the couch and walked down the dirt road to see if Lola and Mannie were ready to go.

EIGHT

Hayride Stories

Stella passed the Zulachs' yellow cabin with the five-man tent set up next to it. She heard the guys carrying on inside the tent, laughing and shouting at each other, and decided to deal with them later.

The last house at the end of the Fish Camp was the Barconis', and it was built into the side of the mountain. The Barconis had four children.

Tillie, the oldest girl at seventeen, was working at a local resort for the summer. Stella didn't know her very well.

The youngest, a boy named Anthony, was four, the same age as the twins.

But Lola and Mannie were only a year apart, close to Stella's age, and they were best friends all summer. Stella never saw them during the school year because they lived in a different part of the valley, but it only took a few days to rekindle the friendship each year.

At the bottom of the steps, Stella yelled, "Hullo, Lola! Hullo, Man-nie!" She waited until Mannie poked her head of long, dark-brown, curly hair out the screened front door. Even though Stella and Mannie were about the same age and same height, Mannie was a lot more developed physically.

She had started to wear a bra last year and really needed it. Her Mama said the Barconi women always developed faster, and Stella shouldn't worry because she would sprout a bosom soon.

Mannie motioned, "Come on in, Stel! Our daddy's putting batteries in the flashlights. We are almost ready."

Stella hopped up the steps and followed Mannie into a large room that was a kitchen in one corner with a counter separating it from the dining and living area. There was one bedroom downstairs and a loft upstairs where all the children slept.

After Stella's father built their Cabin, Stella's mother made such a fuss that he finally made a small indoor bathroom with a toilet, shower stall, and tiny sink. But the Barconis still had to use an outhouse, and they took their baths in a huge oval washtub that otherwise hung on the outside cabin wall.

While Lola was helping Mr. Barconi with the flashlights, Mrs. Barconi yelled out, "Stella, come in the kitchen and taste my cannolis."

Stella rushed right over to the pile stacked on the counter, since Mrs. Barconi made the best cannolis Stella ever ate.

Stella bit into the crunchy crust of a tube-shaped, sugarcoated pastry and savored the filling of ricotta cheese flavored with pistachio and candied cherries.

"Oh, yum, these are wonderful, Mrs. Barconi," she said, wiping the fluffy white sugar around her mouth with the back of her hand; "as usual."

"Oh, I'm glad you like them," she walked around the bar and gave Stella a hug. Mrs. Barconi was a huge woman, the product of her own good cooking. Stella always felt comfortable around her.

Mr. Barconi had the flashlights ready, handed them to Lola, and gave her a pat on the butt. "Go get them crawlers, now! But you girlies be careful out there in the dark, so One Hand Sid don't getcha—woo!"

At thirteen, Lola was older and more mature than Mannie and Stella. She was easily four inches taller than her sister and had cropped dark hair. "We're not afraid, Daddy. We'll just whack him with our flashlights! Stella, what time are we getting back?"

"Harry was saying we'd be out there about two hours, so we should be back around midnight; is that okay, Mrs. Barconi?"

"Oh sure," she waved her apron up and down in front of her face to force a breeze. "I know you girls are safe with your father. He knows his way around this whole county, I think. He won't let you get into trouble. Have fun, and you girls behave, you hear me. I don't want any bad reports."

"Okay, Mama," Lola and Mannie muttered together. "Let's go!"

"Oh, here, Stella; take these few cannoli to your family. I know how much your daddy loves them." And she shoved a full, grease-speckled paper bag into Stella's hands. She wondered if all the delicious desserts would make it to the Cabin.

"Thanks, Mrs. Barconi," Stella called, as she and her friends piled out the front door.

As the girls approached the tent next to the Zulach cabin, Chi-Chi poked his head out the front flap. "Here they come, guys; let's tie them up and tickle 'em."

By the time the girls reached the tent, all three boys were standing outside.

Lester was stuffing his shirt into his shorts. He was about three inches taller than Harry, even though their birthdays were only a few weeks apart. He was skinny like Harry but had a head full of dark curly hair. When they walked together, Stella called them Salt and Pepper because Harry was definitely a towhead. Lester was Harry's best friend in the camp.

His brother Joey was three years younger and acted it. He looked like a smaller, younger version of Lester, but Stella thought they were quite different in attitude.

Lester was sensible, but Joey was the one to jump off the highest point of Indian Rock Ledge or end up getting stuck in the rapids where he shouldn't have gone in the first place.

It seemed Harry and Lester were always getting him out of trouble. Stella thought to herself, I hope he doesn't do anything dumb tonight.

Chi-Chi lived at the other end of the camp and was the same age as Stella and Mannie. They both had a crush on him, and it seemed of all the guys, he was always the one to tease Stella, but other than that, he never seemed to pay much attention to them.

Stella took a deep breath and walked up to the group. In her most authoritative voice she said, "Okay, you rejects. My daddy said we need to be ready by eight, and you each need a flashlight with good batteries. So, we'll see you then. Any questions?" Lola and Mannie giggled in the background.

"NO, SIR!" All three boys mockingly saluted Stella and broke out laughing. Stella laughed with them. She had so much experience minding the twins, these guys were a piece a cake.

She turned, and the three girls ran down the road, before they got further harassed.

When the girls stepped onto the back porch of the Cabin, Peppy was already sleeping on his carpet in the corner. He got up and welcomed them by licking their hands and smelling for the scent of foreign animals.

"Stop, Peppy! Leave us be. Go lie down on your carpet. Good dog." When the dog settled, they went inside.

"Hi, Mrs. Karvotsky. Are you coming on the hayride?" Lola went over and hugged Stella's mama.

"Yeah, I'm riding in the truck, but the twins are riding in the trailer with you. Stella, be sure they stay next to you girls, and do not go near the tailgate; okay?"

Stella's mother was gathering juice and cookies to keep the twins occupied when they got to the golf course, and jackets and blankets so they could sleep.

"Sure, Mama, they'll be okay. Just tell the guys not to throw them out of the trailer if they get on their nerves. You know how they are!"

"Oh Stella, they're not that bad. We might as well lock up and get ready to go. Daddy and the twins are outside already."

"Hey, Stel, can I use your bathroom before we go? One less time I have to use that outhouse. I wish we could put a bathroom in our cabin." Mannie headed for the tiny bathroom that was a closet before Mr. Karvotsky had remodeled it.

"Mama, here, Mrs. Barconi sent some cannoli. I thought about hiding them, but I figured I better be honest." Stella laughed and put the paper bag on the kitchen table.

"Arlene sure is a good cook. I'll save them for later. You know Daddy loves them." Her mother put the bag on top of the silver and black breadbox. "Stella, please go close the side door, and we can go out the back."

When Stella, her mother, and the girls got outside, the boys were standing around the trailer. The twins were trying to climb in from the tailgate. Harry helped them, and everybody else piled in. The hay smelled so sweet and fresh. The twins started throwing it up in the air in handfuls.

"Okay, you two. Let's settle down." Stella positioned them between herself and Lola and Mannie, and the guys shared the rest of the space. Fred and Sophie got into the front, and the truck pulled out of the driveway to the road.

Her father drove along River Road towards town, but before they got to the bridge, he turned right and took the snaking dirt road away from the river. They passed several open pastures, and a few times Fred slowed down so the gang could count the deer grazing in the fields. It was nearly dark, so the deer felt safe and didn't run even when the group yelled to them.

"Oh, there's Bambi!" shouted Elsie. "See him by his mother."

"Oh yeah, there're LOTS of Bambis out there," Harry and Lester smirked knowingly to each other, since both had already been deer hunting for several years.

By now it was practically pitch dark, and Stella's father slowed down at a stop sign. Then he maneuvered across the main highway onto another narrower dirt road that started at a steep incline. Stella heard the truck go into low gear.

She motioned to Mannie, "This is Spooky Road! My dad says there are bear in these woods." The twins hid their heads under Stella's arms.

Everyone spoke in hushed tones, not wanting to rouse the anger of creatures that might be watching. The trees hung scarily overhead, and Stella felt as if they were passing through cobwebs.

Lester told a story about a young girl walking on the dark road, and a farmer stopped to see if she needed help, so she got into his truck and showed him where she lived.

After he dropped her off, he noticed she left her scarf on the seat. So, he went back and knocked on the door.

When a woman came to the door, she saw the scarf and started screaming for her husband, who came running because he thought someone was trying to hurt his wife. But when she showed him the scarf, he stared at it in disbelief.

It was the scarf their only daughter was wearing when she was hit by a car and killed on the same road years ago.

This was the Young Girl Ghost Story that Stella had heard many times, but it always gave her goose bumps, and in this setting, her bumps were big as mosquito bites!

As if the twins weren't already scared out of their wits, Stella just moaned when Chi-Chi brought up the story about One Hand Sid.

The way he told it, a few New York City Mafia groups hung out in the Catskill Mountains about an hour away from the Fish Camp.

"My pa said they ran a gambling operation out of those resorts up there, and Sid "The Shooter" Spamoli was one mean gangster." To Stella's dismay, Chi-Chi was really getting into the story.

"They say that this one weekend, Sid's gang showed up at a resort and stole a bunch of jewelry from a lady; like a diamond bracelet and some family-heirloom ring worth a bunch of money. The crazy part was that the lady was related to the Mafia Boss that ran that resort!"

Stella was getting a little more interested since she hadn't ever heard Chi-Chi's version. "What a mistake that was for Sid!" Chi-Chi continued.

"Sid had enough time to hide the jewelry somewhere in these mountains, but when the Mafia Boss guys finally caught up with him, as punishment for stealing from them, they beat Sid up and cut off his right hand."

At this point, Stella told the twins, "Elsie and Stosh, cover your ears NOW!" The twins immediately obeyed at the sound of Stella's voice.

Chi-Chi finished the story. "It was about a week later that the Sheriff's group found Sid's truck up in Sheepshead Hollow near the Black Pony Inn. But all they found was his dried-up bloody hand on the seat of the truck. The Shooter and the jewels had vanished, and he picked up the name 'One Hand Sid.'"

Harry said, "You know my dad told me after it happened, some gangster-looking customers came to rent a couple of boats and motors one Sunday."

Harry was adding what Stella thought was really the scary part. "They went up the rapids and checked both sides of the river and went into the Cove and around Indian Ledge. It was obvious they were looking for something, or someone, and Dad figured it was their buddy, Sid."

Stella couldn't hold back her fear a minute longer and butted in, "I just wonder what happened to him."

Then Harry added more fuel to the discussion. "Well, I overheard Dad and Mr. Gannett talking to the sheriff about Mr. Gannett's fire."

"It seems someone might have been using Mr. Gannett's barn for a hideout because they found some evidence by the barn that looks suspicious. He might have been the cause of the fire!"

Stella looked over to the twins with their hands still covering their ears and whispered to Lola and Mannie and the guys, "So you think he's still wandering around these woods?"

Harry glanced at her sideways and shrugged his shoulders. Just at that that moment, a breeze shook the overhanging trees, and she felt a rush of cool air rush over them. Lola and Mannie hugged each other tightly.

Stella shivered and rubbed her arms. She shook the twins, who still had their hands against the sides of their faces, and told them, "Okay, you two, you can open your ears."

When the truck and trailer finally reached the top of Shiflin Mountain, the gravel road widened, and the trees no longer clutched the road.

The moon was less than half full but provided enough light to highlight the fields and trees.

Lester pointed out the Big and Small Dipper. He was reading a book about planets and stars because he wanted to be an astronomer one day.

Soon they pulled onto another road, this one paved. The bouncing and jouncing in the trailer stopped, and Fred went faster.

The breeze was almost too cool, and Stella covered the twins with the blanket. Then her father slowed down and turned into the parking lot of the Shiflin Golf Course.

The mountain and the golf course got their name from the people who owned all the land around it.

"We're here! See the sign?" Stella motioned to the group. "Can you believe all this land belongs to the Shiflin's."

Mr. Shiflin's family had settled the mountain over a hundred years ago, and when he died, his son Ellwood P. Shiflin II came home after college and built the golf course.

He had learned to play golf when he was studying at Harvard, and there were not any courses in this area. So, he built one for himself and his rich friends who came to stay at the resort he built.

"My daddy said that Mr. Ellwood Shiflin made a lot of money in "The Market," whatever that means," Stella added, and shook her head. "I'm not sure what they sell in "The Market" but it must be good because he sure is rich."

A chorus of "You said it" and low whistles followed from the group.

Her father knew both Mr. Shiflins. He was friends with Mr. Shiflin Sr. before he died; they used to go hunting together. In fact, he was Fred's hunting partner the day her father shot the bear.

"You know, my dad told me the story about how he shot that bear," Harry told the guys.

"They were on Shiflin Mountain and had not seen hide nor hair of any bear. When it was starting to get dark and they were about ready to head back, Mr. Shiflin noticed piles of bear poop here and there."

Then Harry crouched down and informed the group, "You know, bears poop balls; the size depends on the size of the bear and what they're eating. But a five-hundred-pound bear will poop something the size of a meatball, and Mr. Shiflin and my dad were seeing piles of meatballs all around." He waved his hands to exaggerate the story.

"There are some big huckleberry bushes on the mountain, and my dad was sitting next to one, waiting for Mr. Shiflin to water some bushes. He heard rustling and looked up."

At his point Harry raised himself up and stared at the sky. "And there, right in front of him, is this huge black bear on his hind legs, grabbing and eating dried up huckleberries.

The twins grabbed Stella around her waist and started moaning.

"My dad said he was frozen for a minute, but then scrambled to his feet, picked up his gun, aimed, and shot the bear. When it fell into the bush, he was afraid it would fall on him, because his feet were not working right then."

This brought more moaning and groaning from the guys in the trailer.

"When he heard the shot, Mr. Shiflin ran back from doing his duty and nearly dropped his teeth." Harry sat back down in the trailer, smiling, and satisfied with his storytelling.

Stella's father had killed that bear with one shot in the head. And that was the Big Bear Story!

Stella then added, "You know, they hung that bear off the railing of our front porch for everybody to see."

Harry had to add a bit more information. "When word got around, people came from all over. After a couple of days, our dad had it dressed out at a local butcher. The scale only weighed up to five hundred pounds, and the bear was touching the floor. Can you believe that?" Harry shook his head and that started more moaning from the group.

Stella took a turn at the story. "Everybody in the neighborhood got to eat bear meat. In my opinion, it tasted like pork chops, but the meat was really greasy." She made an unhappy face, as if she had just eaten something bad.

Stella then told the group that her father paid a taxidermist somewhere in Minnesota to preserve the hide, with the head still attached, and the family laid it out on the living-room floor with that snarl on his face, big white teeth, and red gums.

Eventually, their mother put the bearskin in a box with mothballs and stored it in the attic, because when the twins came along, they were always pulling its ears, and it was looking a bit scraggly.

Mr. Shiflin and Stella's father had good times together, hunting and fishing. He always gave Mr. Shiflin a free boat and motor whenever he wanted to fish the river, and in the winter, the family could skate on Mr. Shiflin's lake on the top of the mountain or go ice fishing.

When old Mr. Shiflin died, his son told Fred he could still come anytime and pick night crawlers on the golf course, if they were careful not to mess up the greens.

Young Mr. Shiflin said it was fine if Fred told him when he would be there, so the Security Guard wouldn't shoot them, thinking they were bears or looters.

NINE

Night Crawlers

Fred slowed down and braked in the parking lot of Mr. Shiflin's golf course, and everybody piled out of the trailer. Harry handed out the cans that Stella and her daddy had prepared. Sophie had her own flashlight, so she took the twins to sit by the pool house to eat their snack.

Her father gave everyone a general layout of the course area and where we could go. He looked at his watch. "Gang, it's a few minutes before nine. When I blow the horn twice, that's the signal to head back. Okay?"

Harry was the first to respond. "Sounds good, Dad."

The guys shared high fives in response and headed in one direction. They spread out, their flashlights sweeping the ground.

Stella, Mannie, and Lola headed in the opposite direction. Mannie and Lola had only looked for night crawlers on the lawns at the Fish Camp and had never come to the golf course before.

"Wait until you see how many there are and how easy it is to catch them here."

Stella whispered, so the earthworms wouldn't get scared away. She slipped the handle of the can over her left arm and held the flashlight in that hand. Then she bent down and followed the light as she scanned the close-cropped golf course grass in front of her. To her right, she saw the thin snaky outline of a worm spread out across the grass.

"The trick is to figure out which end of the worm is near or partly in the hole," she told her friends. She slammed the edge of her hand down on the worm, not so hard as to hurt the creature, but firm enough it would not wiggle away.

Sure enough, she guessed right, and one end of the worm was still in the hole, while the other end waved wildly under her hand. She gently pulled the loose end, and the rest of the night crawler sprang out.

"Gotcha! I got my first one," Stella called to the other girls in a hushed voice. "Ninety-nine more to go." She plunked it into her bucket.

"I just got one too!" Mannie called to the others.

"Me too. I just got a double! This is a great place to get 'em," Lola sounded excited.

Stella knew what a double was. Night crawlers are not males or females; they're actually both. There is a strange name for that called a hermaphrodite. What happens when two night crawlers come out of their holes and they want to mate, they lay next to each other real close and fertilize each other.

The good thing is when they are so close, you can put down the can, hold the flashlight under your chin, and use both hands to pinch them so neither one can get back in their hole. And you can catch two for the price of one!

One time, Stella even saw three in a row!

Picking was good, and after an hour or more Stella needed only ten more to reach her goal of a hundred. She was so involved in her goal that she wasn't paying close attention to where the flashlight took her.

When she stood up to give her back a rest and look around, she noticed the other flashlights were extremely far away. Hers was the only light out there, close to the edge of the woods.

Suddenly she heard rustling coming from the darkened tree line! It was rhythmic, like someone, or something, was walking in the woods. Her heart beat against her chest wall and pounded in her ears.

"Who's there?" She yelled in the direction of the rustling noise. "Is that you, Harry?" "Chi-Chi?" The noise stopped suddenly. All she could hear now were peep frogs and crickets.

She picked up her can, turned, and ran as fast as she could to where other lights were scanning the ground. She came up to closest one which ended up being Harry.

"What is wrong with you. Stel?" Harry was upset with his sister. "You want to scare every worm on this course back in its hole?"

He shined the light onto Stella's face and saw her expression and heavy breathing and the beads of sweat on her forehead. "What was chasing you?" He waved his flashlight behind her but saw nothing.

Stella took a few deep breaths and said, "I accidentally got close to the woods and heard something like someone walking through the leaves. It did not sound like an animal. I thought maybe it was you guys trying to scare me. So, I called out, but no one answered, and the noise stopped. Then I started running."

"What would a person be doing in those woods at night?"

Then as an afterthought he added, "Unless it was One Hand Sid, woo!" He waved his flashlight under his chin to shine on his face.

"I'm sure it was an animal, but that could have had a bad ending too. Good thing you ran back."

"Harry, I know it was not an animal. If it was, it walked on two feet!" Stella was convinced.

"Look, you can hang around me if you want, until we finish. I got over two hundred already, and I think we're about to hear that horn blow to go back." He turned away from Stella and bent down to scan the ground.

Stella breathed a huge sigh of relief. She moved a short way from her brother, keeping his light in view for the rest of the time.

Soon, her father blew the horn twice, and all the flashlights slowly moved in his direction.

When everyone got back, Fred put the cans of worms in the back of the truck and covered them with a towel so they couldn't get out. "Well, how was it picking out there, gang?" Fred asked the group.

Another chorus of oohs and ahhs came from the pickers.

Sophie and the twins were sleeping on the truck seat. The twins woke up as soon as they heard the activity and headed for Stella.

When the worm-pickers all climbed back into the trailer, her father slammed the tailgate shut and leaned on it.

"You did so good tonight, Ma and I decided we'll stop for a treat on the way back. Is everybody up for ice cream?" He got yeahs and hurrahs from the crowd.

* * *

When they pulled into the parking lot of Fern Lake Grill, the outside lights hurt their eyes until they got adjusted. The gang discussed what they would order.

Harry whispered in Lester's ear, "I'm getting the dipped chocolate cone, you know, an SOS." Both boys chuckled to themselves.

But Stosh and Elsie, using the super hearing of three-year-olds, overheard the "SOS" word and started oohing and aahing, "Stel-la, Harry said a bad word!"

"Oh, be quiet, you twin pains in the butt!" Harry yelled at them and continued to tell Lester, "They make it with real chocolate here, and you can have any flavor of ice cream."

Stella piped in, "Yeah, those are good, but I want a strawberry sundae, with nuts."

When they arrived at the Grill, everyone washed their hands at the outside faucet and piled into the diner.

It was such a big group, they took up all the shiny chrome barstools with soft red leather seats that lined the bar.

Josie, the waitress, took their orders one at a time.

Harry went first. "Josie, I want an SOS with chocolate ice cream, please."

"One SOS coming up!" Josie shouted and winked at Harry. She filled a cone with soft chocolate ice cream and then expertly flipped it upside down into a stainless-steel canister of melted chocolate. When she pulled it out, the cold ice cream immediately froze the chocolate, and she handed it to Harry.

"Who's next?" Josie leaned on the counter.

The twins wanted what Harry had, but Sophie made them get their ice cream in a cup because she knew it would make the least mess.

By the time everyone had eaten their treats, it was nearly midnight, which was the summer closing time for the Grill.

When Fred paid the bill, everyone piled into the trailer one last time.

The twins wanted to be wrapped in the blanket in the trailer because the ice cream made them cold, and they were asleep again before her father got the truck into high gear.

Everybody sang on the way home. "Old McDonald Had a Farm," using all the animals they could think of, and they were all the way down to Five Bottles of Beer on the Wall, as they bounced down the dirt path to the Fish Camp.

When Stella opened the back-porch door to help her mother get the twins into the Cabin, Peppy bolted out the door and headed for the woods.

Sophie's eyes followed him in surprise. "Poor Peppy, he really had to go." Stella remembered that Harry had fed the dog golumbki juice, but kept her mouth shut.

When she came back out to say goodnight to Mannie and Lola, her father had already paid everyone for their pickings, and Harry and the guys had combined all the worms into their new home in the cellar.

In total, the group had caught over eight-hundred-night crawlers!

Her father was really pleased. Now he wouldn't have to buy any from "that weasel in Cohocton." But it looked like Stella would be doing the dishes alone next week since Harry won the bet of getting the most crawlers!

Harry, Lester, Chi-Chi, and Joey headed toward the tent after their review of tomorrow's plans.

Lola and Mannie shined their flashlights in front of them and headed home. Stella watched the lights disappear down the road.

She called Peppy, and together they went into the Cabin and latched the porch door.

TEN

July 4th Firemen's Celebration

On Monday morning, Stella was awake, listening to early-morning sounds, but she deliberately didn't open her eyes. She had slept on the screened porch, which was Harry's summer bedroom. Harry had spent the last few nights with his friends in the tent, so Stella got to sleep in her favorite bed.

The porch was screened on three sides, and her father had attached huge, hinged plywood shutters to cover the screens when the weather was cold. Stella liked to sleep with the shutters propped up, so the breeze from the river with its smells of wet rock and plants would wash over her through the night.

As she lay in bed last night, covered up to her eyes with the warm, soft pierzyna, she could see the stars and eventually fell asleep to night songs of whippoorwills and crickets.

The porch faced the river, so this morning Stella could hear the faint roar of the rapids upstream. Stella thought about how much you can know without opening your eyes

She breathed in deeply through her nose. Her mother was cooking breakfast. The smell of bacon and eggs mixed with fresh-perked coffee made Stella's stomach rumble.

She heard voices in the Fish Camp and thought she could hear Mr. Zulach down by the river, calling Lester.

Occasionally, she would hear a car pass on River Road above the camp.

Stella finally opened her eyes and stretched the full length of the bed. She traced the metal filigree at the foot of the bed with the tip of her big toe and barely touched the headboard with her fingertips.

Now she knew for sure she'd grown at least one inch since the beginning of summer because she could never stretch the full length of this bed before!

I can't believe today is already the Fourth of July, Stella thought. School had been out for only a month, but she always felt that after July 4th, the gloom of leaving the Fish Camp and returning to school hung thick in the air.

July 4th holiday was always her favorite, next to Christmas. The Fish Camp was at full throttle. All the cabins were rented, so the camp was filled with old and new friends, and the die-hard fishermen had boats reserved for weeks in advance.

Harry, Stella, and their mother helped to prepare fish bait, and her father cut the grass around the cabins and even down the bank to the river.

Everybody prayed for clear weather because this was the day her father made the most money from the Fish Camp.

And Stella knew this year her parents had to make enough to pay off that loan for the Cabin.

Stella slid out from the warm bed and saw there was still a thin cloud of fog hovering over the water all the way to the bend in the river. Usually this meant a blue sky by late morning.

She thought about today's schedule. First, get all the fishermen on the water and check on the renters in their cabins.

Around lunchtime, she and Harry would row across the river to the Firemen's Celebration at the municipal airport.

Stella had saved almost ten dollars from picking bait for her father and the tips from helping the fishermen, and she was planning on how she would spend it on games, rides, and candy.

She definitely wanted to ride the Ferris Wheel again this year. Last year when her car reached the top of the wheel, she could see the Fish Camp and the river all the way to the Bridge! It was a little scary, but fun.

She could almost taste the candied apple that she would buy and the sweet fluffy ball of pink cotton candy.

When she and Harry would get back to the Fish Camp later that afternoon, her mother would drive them to Aunt Sarah and Uncle Josh's farm a few miles down River Road.

They would pick the first fresh sweet corn of the season and bring it back to cook with hot dogs and chicken on the outside fireplace.

And when darkness fell, the Fireman's Celebration across the river would guarantee that the Fish Camp porches had first-class seats for the best fireworks in the area!

Stella smiled and knew this would be a good day.

When Stella pranced into the kitchen, face washed and dressed, her father was sitting at one end of the white rectangular kitchen table that was covered with red-and-white checkered vinyl. He was calculating something from the Cabin receipt book. Her mother was pouring coffee into mugs.

"Well, how is the Fish Camp's champion bait catcher doing this morning?" Her father closed the book and looked up at Stella.

She ran over and sat on one knee of his lap and rested her head against his chest. It was so nice to have her dad here. This was the only week of the summer he took vacation to stay at the Fish Camp.

"I'm great, and ready to go to the Firemen's Celebration. Are you and Mama going this year?"

Her mother put the speckled-blue coffeepot back on the stove and sat across from her father.

"I'll drive over with the twins after lunch for the parade and let them ride the pony and a few of the kiddie rides."

Then her mother added, in a rather stern tone, "Stella, we're letting you go with Harry, and we want you to stay together. No wandering off by yourself. And if you want to go with me to pick corn, you two better be back here by four."

Her mother got up from the table and went to the kitchen counter. She brought back a plate of bacon, eggs and toast and laid it on the table opposite Fred. "Now sit down and eat your breakfast."

Fred patted Stella on the butt and sent her to her chair. He squeezed his thick black eyebrows together and tilted his head toward Stella from across the table

. "You be sure to listen to Harry. Those gambling booths over there seem to attract strange folks from the city, and you need to stay together. I don't want to have to go looking for you in New York City!"

Stella smiled and said, "Oh, don't worry, Daddy. We will be careful. And we will definitely be back by four, so please don't leave without us, Mama. I want to see the twin goats Daddy helped Uncle Josh deliver last weekend. What did he name them, Daddy?"

Her father scratched his head, "I'm not sure, Nan and Dan or Mel and Nell. The second one sure had a tough time, but I think she'll make it okay. Her right ear is a little crooked from us pulling on her to get her born, but I think it'll straighten out."

Stella imagined a baby goat with a crooked ear and laughed to herself. *Nan and Dan, Mel and Nell. I could think of better names than those.*

Stella had already finished breakfast and was helping her mother get the twins dressed and ready when Harry staggered into the kitchen, black shadows under his eyes and his blonde cowlick sticking straight up. It was obvious he did not get much sleep.

"Oh, and what did you guys do all night instead of sleeping?" His mother hugged his shoulders and walked him to a seat. He slumped down and put his head on the table.

"Well, Chi-Chi taught Lester and me a new game of cards called Aces, and we played it until after midnight. And then we talked. Till about four, I think."

Stella leaned over and smelled Harry's shirt. "And you smoked rabbit tobacco all night too, I bet!" She loved getting him into trouble sometimes.

Harry shoved her away and indignantly brushed himself off. "Noo, we didn't smoke rabbit tobacco, Miss Know It All! And who made YOU Hall Monitor?"

Their father muffled a laugh, and Sophie said, "Alright you two. Harry, eat your breakfast so you can help Daddy get those boats ready. Stella, keep an eye on the twins while I check out the cabins to make sure they have enough sheets and towels. Then you two can head over to the Celebration."

Her mother walked over to a jar in the corner of the kitchen where she kept money from bait sales and pulled out a few bills.

"I'm sure you would rather have one of their hamburgers and lemonade for lunch. Here are a few dollars, so you don't have to spend your own money for that. Now, let's get going!"

* * *

Harry and Stella jumped into the only boat that hadn't been rented because it was a leaker. Stella untied the boat and shoved off from the dock.

"Geez, Harry. I just bailed the water out of here about an hour ago. It sure is leaking bad!"

"Ah, don't worry. We won't sink," Harry just laughed.

With a few strong pulls, he turned the boat to face the opposite shore and with even strokes made his way across the river while Stella bailed the rest of the water from the boat.

Then she leaned over and examined the clear bottom of the river. She saw several lamprey eel nests.

Her father told Stella lampreys are among the oldest fishes on earth, and she was fascinated by the stories of how they migrate from the rivers to and from the sea.

She and her family had visited relatives in New Jersey one time, and she knew the ocean was far away from this river. She hoped the fishermen would tell the lamprey story again tonight during the cookout by the fire.

When Harry rowed close enough to the opposite shore, Stella stood ready and jumped off. She pulled the bow of the boat onto the rocky edge and tied the line to a pine-tree branch that hung close to the water.

Harry jumped out and pulled the boat higher on the rocky shore to slow down the leak, checked Stella's knot, and together they climbed the dirt path to the top of the riverbank.

Stella could hear the fiddle music and laughter and sweet smell of burnt sugar from the cotton-candy stand. They walked along the path made by previous campers and hikers but couldn't pass by early bearing huckleberry bushes without tasting a handful of the ripe berries.

Finally, they entered the open field of the municipal airport to meet the Midway of the Fair.

"Let's get lunch, Stella, and then I want to try my luck at the dart game. Last year I won that big pink elephant, remember?"

Stella and Harry ordered hamburgers "all the way" and fresh-squeezed lemonade from the St. Peter's Auxiliary group. Suzanna's family were members of St. Peter's Church, and she was working at the booth with Mrs. Gannett.

"Hi, Suzanna," Stella said and hugged her. "Do you want to come over and watch the fireworks with us tonight?"

"Oh, I'd love to, but my parents asked me to watch with them here after we finish our shift at the stand. Maybe I could do that next year. Are you still coming to the barn to ride tomorrow? My mom was going to drop me off about nine."

"For sure. I'll be there by nine." Stella happily responded.

Mrs. Gannett handed Stella and Harry their burgers, and then with a smile, gave them a free order of fries.

"Oh wow, Mrs. Gannett! Thank you." Then Stella smothered them with ketchup.

Harry and Stella wandered the Midway where Harry tried his luck throwing darts. The chances were three for a quarter, and he didn't get anything the first round. On the next quarter, though, he broke three of the balloons in a row, and the barker in the striped suit yelled, "A Winner! We got us a winner!" He told Harry to pick something from the top shelf of the prizes.

"What should I pick, Stel? What do you think Terry would like?"

"I think she would like that brown teddy bear, Harry. Get that!" Stella was excited for her brother. When he took his prize, they moved off down the Midway.

"Now, remember, Dad said to stay with me," Harry warned Stella. "I don't want it to be my fault for you getting picked up by some freak here, okay?"

"No problem, Harry. I don't want to get kidnapped either!"

Just then, they heard a low roaring in the sky and knew exactly what was happening. At two o'clock sharp, every Fourth of July, weather permitting, the amazing Blue Angels would appear to shock the crowd.

When the four synchronized jet planes made their first pass over the airfield, the noise was so loud, Stella covered her ears, but she could still feel the vibration in her bones! Harry's eyes followed every movement of the planes.

"Oh man, look at them go! Now they're going to do the bridge, I'll bet!" Stella and Harry ran as fast as they could to the clearing in the trees, where you could see the Darbytown Bridge that crossed the river.

"Here they come!" Harry yelled. "Oh jeez, look at them." One by one they maneuvered the jet planes underneath the span of the bridge. "Man, that's one dangerous stunt, Stel." Harry just shook his head. "Leave it to the Blue Angels, they're the best!"

After the planes made their last pass over the airfield, Harry and Stella did pay to see the two-headed cow and watched the Fat Lady wind a boa constrictor around her body. But Harry deliberately guided his sister away from a few sideshows.

"Stel, I'm going to see the stunt plane rides. Do you want to come with me?"

But Stella did not want to join him. "I know Mama and Daddy said we must stay together but could I just stay here in the barn and look at the animals, please? I won't go anywhere else." Stella begged Harry. She didn't really want to see any more airplanes today.

"Okay but stay right here. I will come get you about three-thirty, so we can row home in time to go to Uncle Josh's." Then he ran off to the airfield.

Stella wandered about the exhibit barn, petting rabbits, and admiring multi-colored chickens. She was near a beehive exhibit when she overheard two men talking.

"Yeah, The Boss knows The Shooter was up at Shiflin Mountain a couple of days ago," a man dressed in a New York City suit was saying to another guy, who also dressed like he was from The City.

"They didn't get him, though. He was lucky again. There are a lot of mountains up here to get lost in, for sure." He slapped the other guy on the back, and they walked out of the exhibit barn.

Stella was frozen in her tracks. "The Shooter, Shiflin Mountain, a few days ago, when we were picking nightcrawlers!" Stella's heart seemed to stop at the thought.

She looked around to see if anyone saw how close she was to those men. Then, as calm as she could make herself, she walked to the opposite side of the barn. When she glanced at her watch, it said 3:33. Mama was leaving at four, and Harry was nowhere in sight.

She left the animal exhibit and headed to the airfield. Stella searched for his blonde head in the crowd around a biplane. Finally, she spied him!

ELEVEN

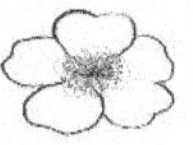

Aunt Sarah and Uncle Josh

Stella had to coax her brother away from the airfield where a stunt pilot was giving airplane rides for five dollars in his yellow fabric-covered biplane. It had a beautiful sunset painted on the wings.

She ran up to him and shook him by the shoulders. "Harry, Harry, we got to go! It is almost 4 o'clock." She pointed to her Cinderella watch and waved it in his face.

She knew Harry wanted that ride into the heavens as he watched the takeoff and landings. He told her later he could feel the lump in his stomach when the plane banked in and out of turns and wished, just wished, each time it could be his ride.

But he had promised his parents he would not, absolutely not, get into that airplane—with threats of permanent grounding, and having to do dinner dishes for the rest of his life!

"Oh man, the time just flew by" he said and grabbed her arm and pulled her toward the path to the river.

Harry and Stella practically ran down the slope of riverbank, leaving the sounds and smells of the Firemen's July 4th Picnic fading in the background.

Harry held on tightly to the brown bear he had won for Terry. Stella slid down the last turn of the dirt path leading to the rocky edge of the river.

"Here, Stel, hold onto Terri's bear for me while I get the boat off the rocks." Harry pushed the bear into Stella's arms.

"I sure hope Mama hasn't gone to Aunt Sarah and Uncle Josh's without us," she said out of breath.

"It's way after four already, and I thought I would NEVER find you in that crowd around the airplane!"

"I'll tell you; next year I WILL ride in that airplane!" Harry untied the line from the tree and started pushing the boat into the water. "Dad already told me that next year he'd go with me."

Stella mumbled to herself, trying to understand the attraction of flying, and hopped into the boat. Harry jumped into the boat, set the oars, and started pulling them through the water.

"Good job on pulling the boat up high on shore, Harry. There's not even enough water for me to need to bail. I'll just hold on to this cute bear." Stella almost wished it was hers.

Within a few minutes Harry had rowed back to the other side. Stella jumped out before the boat hit the dock and tied it to a cleat. "I'm gonna make sure Mama didn't leave without us."

She didn't even wait for Harry but ran up the wooden steps to the top of the riverbank.

Her chest heaving from the run, she gasped for air as she reached the top of the bank and looked up to meet the face of her mother.

"Good thing you two got here now. I was going to leave, but I saw you barreling down the bank on the other side. Lucky you didn't fall and break your neck." She said to Stella. "Lucky you're a tomboy!" She turned, shook her head, and headed toward the car.

Stella realized she was still holding onto the brown bear and threw it to Harry as he got to the top of the stairs. "Here's your prize for Terri."

"Thanks. I'll meet you at the car as soon as I put this in my room." Then Stella headed in the direction of her mother.

Elsie and Stosh were already sitting in the backseat, each holding a small red box of Animal Crackers covered with circus animals.

"Look, Stella!" Stosh yelled as Stella opened the car door. "I'm going to eat this tiger! Roaraahh!" He pushed a cracker into her face and then into his mouth.

"And I got a bear, Stella, look," shouted Elsie. She swallowed the cracker and then dug into the box and pulled out another. "You want one? Here's a Jerf." Elsie shoved a cracker at Stella as she got into the backseat.

"It's called a gir-affe, Elsie," she sounded out the name for her little sister. "Did you two have a good ride on the pony at the Fair?"

The twins, excited, shouted at the same time, "Yeah!"

Harry jumped into the front seat and slammed the door. "Sorry we were a little late, Ma. I just had to watch that biplane a few more times. Could you see it over the trees? He gave one guy the ride of his life! They did a loop; oh man, I wish I could have been in that plane!"

"Oh, yes, I could see the plane from here. And every time it took off, I wondered whether you were going to keep your promise." His mother looked sternly at her son.

"Ma, I promised you I would not ride this year, so I didn't. But next year must be different. Dad said so."

Her mother gave a deeply concerned, motherly sigh, started the engine, and slowly chugged up the dirt road out of the Fish Camp. At the top of the road, instead of turning left to town, she turned right onto the narrow river road and headed north.

A short distance down the road, the twins yelled in unison, "There's Peter Pan Rock. Can you see Tinkerbelle, Stella?"

They all craned their necks as they passed by a large gray lichen-covered rock, shoved by the forces of nature next to a tall oak.

The rock was about four feet high and twice as wide. At the base was a crevice about twelve inches tall, and this was the home of Tinkerbelle.

All the kids in the Fish Camp knew the story and the details. Stella remembered the Peter Pan idea came about because there was a wild grapevine growing in an oak and intertwined at the top of it.

The kids could walk up the rocky hill into the woods, grab hold of the vine, and swing down over the rock, almost like Peter Pan.

Stella was already too old to play the game, but the twins were just starting to add their own twist to the story, so she just kept pretending with them.

Following the curves and turns of the river, the road began to wind. With the windows down, you could smell the wet rocks and foliage as they drove across the wooden one-lane bridge built over a creek that eventually fed into the river.

"Thump, thump," the tires sounded as they bounced over the rough-hewn boards. From the open window, Stella could hear rushing water and knew it came from a small waterfall that dumped into a rocky pool.

"Stosh and Elsie, see that pool by the waterfall. Someday I will take you there and we can look for tadpoles and small minnows. There are really a lot in that spot."

On the other side of the road was a well house that Stella's family had used as their freshwater source when her father first started building the cabins.

Stella could not remember the first cabin being built, although she had seen pictures of herself, about the age of the twins, standing next to her father, with the framework of the cabin in the background.

But she did remember getting buckets and jugs of water from the well with her mother. It was the best tasting water in the world with just a hint of rock and trees. She couldn't explain it any better.

"Hey Stella," chimed Stosh. "Is that the well where we used to get our water?"

Stella smiled at her younger brother. "Yep, Mama and I used to carry pails and jugs of that water to the Cabin before Daddy had our well dug."

Once over the bridge the road curved along the fence of the pasture where Suzanna kept Misty and Sully. They passed the red barn where the horses stayed, and she saw them standing close together under a tree, head to tail, swishing flies from each other's face.

The twins scrambled to the open back window and yelled, "Hi, Mist-y! Hi, Sull-y!" Sully turned her neck and nickered in response.

Along River Road they discussed landmarks. They passed another fish camp with a few trailers instead of cabins.

Harry pointed out the new eel rack out in shallow riffles of the river, where Mr. Snyder would trap the grown eels in wooden chutes he built in the fastest running water.

The eels would get trapped as they made their way back downstream, trying to get to the sea. Mr. Snyder would smoke the eels and sell them in New York City. Stella's mother said people that came from Europe loved them.

There was a straight stretch in the road as they passed a chicken farm, and Harry warned everyone to take a deep breath because of the smell.

"Oh man, those chickens are bad today!" He pinched his nose and rolled up the window on his side.

The twins both carried on, making cackling sounds and pee-yewing noises, until Stella lightly popped each of them on the head.

As they drove up the last hill before Aunt Sarah and Uncle Josh's, her mother stepped on the gas and yelled "Hold On" and they shot over the top.

The twins bounced up in the backseat, almost hitting the ceiling of the car with their heads. Everyone yelled and whooped!

At the bottom of the hill, Sophie slowed down and turned right onto a dirt driveway and pulled up at the back porch of a faded clapboard farmhouse. She beeped the horn twice.

Stella knew Aunt Sarah and Uncle Josh were not related by blood to the family. But when her father first started to build the cabin, Uncle Josh stopped by on his way home from town one day and told her father if he needed anything he would be glad to help and even invited Fred to their house for dinner.

After that dinner, Stella's parents started to help Aunt Sarah and Uncle Josh as much as they could because they did not have many relatives. And from that time on, the families were related.

* * *

The screen door of the clapboard house squeaked open, and out stepped Aunt Sarah. She was a tall, stocky woman with a big, round head covered with short curly salt-and-pepper hair.

She always wore a long print dress that nearly touched the ground. And she was never without an apron of a contrasting color.

Her shoes were the kind Stella's grandmother wore, with a block heel and tiny perforations in the leather that formed spirals, stars, and snowflakes.

Aunt Sarah had a smile and a laugh that could warm the world, and now, as everyone piled out of the car, she shrieked her high-pitched laugh at the joy of seeing everyone and walked towards the family with open arms.

"Oh Sophie! You brought my favorite twins, and my beautiful girl Stella!"

She gathered Stella up into her huge bosom, and Stella got lost in the cleavage and the scent of lavender.

When Aunt Sarah finally released her, Stella felt dizzy for a moment, stepped away from the suffocating bosom, and smiled back.

Harry jumped out of the car as soon as his mother stopped.

"Hi, Aunt Sarah, I'm going down to the barn to find Uncle Josh. Happy Fourth of July!"

Harry hated those hugs; he told Stella it made him feel uncomfortable.

"Aunt Sarah, how are the baby goats doing?" Stella asked, smoothing her hair after Aunt Sarah's hug.

"Oh, sweetheart, the kids are growing like weeds. Thank the Lord for your father, helping Uncle Josh! You want to see them?"

"Yes, ma'am," Stella said.

"Go out to the barn. Uncle Josh is there. Take those little sweeties with you, after I give them kisses." She walked over to Stosh and Elsie and gave them each a hug and kisses. Stosh wiped his kisses off, but Elsie just laughed.

"Let's go, guys! Mama, I'll help you with the corn when you're ready, okay?" Stella grabbed the twins and headed toward the barn.

"Go ahead. I'll track you down when we start picking," her mother yelled as Stella and the twins ran down the path.

* * *

Uncle Josh and Harry were huddled together in a pen inside the barn. When Stella and the twins got close enough, she could see the tiny white goats running around inside.

The mother of the baby goats didn't seem to mind the company; she kept munching on her hay. The goat kids were playing, running around, and chasing each other. Stella noticed the smaller one had a crooked ear. She thought it sure was funny looking.

"Hi, Uncle Josh!" Stella said. "How are you? And the kids?" She smiled and walked over and hugged the tall slender farmer in his faded blue coveralls.

Uncle Josh looked older than Aunt Sarah and had a flowing gray beard and long gray hair. He always wore a huge brown hat. Stella had never seen him take it off.

"Hello, my dear. And look who you brought, my favorite twin people, Mr. Stosh, and Miss Elsie!" He knelt to their level and shook their hands. They giggled at the special adult attention.

Stella, Stosh, and Elsie petted the baby goats. As Stella hugged their necks, the smell reminded her of the twins when Mama first brought them home from the hospital. It was a "new" smell.

Harry and Uncle Josh went to check with Sophie about the corn, and soon Harry came back into the barn. "Ma says we need to get the corn picked and get back on the road. You ready, Stel?"

Stella hated to leave the playful kids. "Yeah, guess we better get going. Come on, you two." Stella separated the twins from the baby goats, and they all left the barn and walked up the path to the cornfield.

Sophie was already picking corn. "Stella and Harry, you can pull some, but make sure you pick the ripe ones. The tassel must be brown, and the husk needs to feel full, okay. We do not want to waste any of Uncle Josh's corn."

"Okay, Mama," Stella said. She examined corn stalks, selected an ear she thought was ready, and pulled it from the stock with a snap.

"What about this one, Mama?" Stella handed it to her mother.

Her mother pulled a strip away at the top and looked at the kernels. "Yes, Stella, this ear of corn is perfect. Pick a dozen just like it."

Stella picked her dozen and put them in the sack Uncle Josh had given her. They took all the corn to the car and loaded it into the trunk.

Aunt Sarah came out of the house to say goodbye. She was carrying a bundle of freshly picked spearmint. "Here, Sophie, steep this to make some spearmint tea. It will help you get through this holiday. I know how hard you work."

"Thank you, Sarah. I'll come later this week to help you put up some corn," Stella's mother replied.

"Oh, my dear, you and Fred are so good to us. You are truly sent from Above. We appreciate all your help. Enjoy the corn roast tonight." They hugged, and the children all piled back into the car.

TWELVE

July 4th Grand Finale!

Stella's mother backed the car between two cabins until it was a few feet from the picnic table. Stella and Harry unloaded the corn from the trunk and piled it on the table.

Her father and three of the fishermen gathered round the cinder-block fireplace at the edge of the riverbank.

They had collected a huge pile of wood along the river left after the ice jam last winter and dumped it close to the roaring fire.

Now they were drinking beer and trading fish stories.

"Hey Larry, can you help me get this on the grill?" Fred dragged out a huge metal sign with a picture of the red flying Texaco horse and Mr. Ward helped him put it on top of the cinder blocks.

Her father yelled to Sophie, "Just in time. We're ready for the corn. Harry, fill the bushel basket with corn, and drag it over here. Stella, grab the burlap bags from the cellar, and bring a bucket of water, too." Her father was good at giving orders.

Her mother headed towards the Cabin. "I'll get the hotdogs and buns. Fred, did you cut the branches so the kids could cook the wieners?"

"Oh yes, I have them ready, right here on the picnic table. How are Josh and Sarah doing? Are those baby goats growing?"

Stella's mother stopped and turned back to her husband with a look of concern. "Well, Josh was a little slow today. His arthritis was kicking up, and he was hurting, but Sarah was her same ole jolly self."

Sophie picked up a pile of the corn from the trunk and dumped it on the picnic table. "And Stella said those goats are so cute! I thought she would never get the twins away from them. Overall, they are doing okay.'

Sophie brought another armful of corn to the table. "The corn is beautiful. No worms and just enough rain. They've got their SWEET CORN sign out, and I think they'll do okay this year."

Fred helped his wife get the rest of the corn out of the trunk and closed the hatch. "They're good people." He added.

"I promised to drive over one day and help Sarah put up some corn for all of us. I think she would appreciate the help, and since you'll still be here on vacation, you can babysit the fishermen for a change."

She let out a laugh, headed to the back porch, and came back in a few minutes with a tray full of dogs, buns, and fixings.

Fred dipped the fresh-picked ears of corn, a few at a time, into the bucket of water Stella brought him and laid them on the metal sheet.

By this time, it was glowing red hot, and the corn steamed and popped when it hit the surface. Fred put about five dozen ears, row to row, next to each other, and then soaked some burlap bags in water. He laid the wet burlap on top of the corn.

Some of the fishermen were real city slickers, and they watched Stella's father start the corn roasting with a lot of interest.

Fred turned to the group behind him and said, "I'll turn them in about fifteen minutes, and we'll be ready to eat by the time the sun goes down. Here, Stella, get me another bucket of water, so we can keep the burlap soaked good. It's the steam that does the cooking."

Stella dragged the bucket of water to her father and tracked down her mama, who was getting the sticks for the twins to cook their hot dogs.

"Mama, are we going to make mickies too?" Mickies are what Stella knew as potatoes thrown into the red-hot coals of the fire until they blackened from being cooked in the coals.

But when you took them out, cut them open, and slathered the inside with real butter, the taste was like nothing else!

"Sure, Stella. Get the bag of potatoes from the back porch. I bought that extra bag just for mickies. Rinse them off in the back-porch sink, though I don't know how much good it does after you burn them to a crisp. But wash them anyway."

Sophie called her son away from the group of fishermen. "Harry, can you bring the watermelon from the fridge on the porch? It should be cold enough by now. And find the big, straight-edge knife with the wooden handle from the kitchen, so we can cut it up."

She corralled the twins and sat them down at the picnic table. "Stosh and Elsie, I am going to let you cook your own hotdogs, BUT you must let me help you!

Sophie gathered the sticks to use for cooking the hot dogs. "And don't go sticking those branches into the fire and waving them around. That's what we have sparklers for later.

"Here, let me help you get the dogs on the sticks." She poked the dogs through their sticks one at a time.

After Sophie slid a hotdog on each of the twins' branches, she positioned them at a safe distance from the fire. She tried to show them how to twist the branch in a circle to cook the dog evenly.

Stosh did a decent job, but Elsie stuck her dog into the coals, and it burned awhile before Sophie could get the fire out.

Elsie whined about eating it, but her mother scraped the charcoal off the end, stuck it into a bun, and muttered, "A little burnt won't hurt you, so just put some ketchup on, and eat it."

Stella overheard her mother talking to the twins and thought, *I think Mama needs to brew herself some of Aunt Sarah's calming spearmint tea about now.*

* * *

The sun had set over the mountain behind the Fish Camp. Its last golden rays sparkled in the ripples on the water and finally faded into darkness.

The activity in the Fish Camp had settled and all that remained now was the occasional splash of a fish breaking water and the deep-throated croaking of a bullfrog looking for his sweetheart.

Stella's father had strung multicolored plastic lanterns along the edge of the porch, and the colored lights reminded her of Christmas without cold.

They could hear the music and noise from the Firemen's Picnic Celebration on the other side of the river. Now and then, a stray firework would go off somewhere in the Fish Camp, and there would be sudden screaming and yelling.

Stella's father pulled the burlap away for the last time, and she breathed in the smell of fresh roasted corn. Using some rusty tongs, he piled the steaming ears, the outside now cooked to a pale yellow, onto a piece of plywood and carried them to the picnic table.

Sophie unwrapped an entire pound of real butter and plopped it onto a plate. With leather gloves, Fred peeled back the yellow shuck from the cobs, but left them attached so you could hold the corn without burning your fingers. Then he handed them out to the crowd.

Stella asked her father to take the shuck off hers. She stuck two miniature, plastic corns with pointed ends into each end.

She rolled the ear over and through the butter until it dripped with sweet yellow oil, salted it, and went over to the swing near the fireplace.

When she bit into the tiny kernels shaped like pearls, they exploded with sweet juice that covered her cheeks and nose.

Four ears of corn, two hotdogs, a mickie, and three toasted marshmallows later, Stella was stuffed! She sat on the edge of the picnic table twirling a roasted marshmallow on the end of a stick.

"Harry, I am full. Do you want this one?"

"Sure, I have room for one more, but that is about it for me. I ate three mickies and a bunch of hotdogs, and I stopped counting the corn." Harry squeezed the hot, melted marshmallow off the end of the stick and stuffed it into his mouth.

"Mama, what time is it?" Stella asked her mother.

"It's about ten minutes to nine, honey. They will be starting the fireworks anytime now."

Stella heard the voice of someone coming around the front of the Cabin, out of the darkness. "Hey Stel, we brought a blanket to sit on!" Mannie and Lola came over to watch the fireworks with Stella.

"Hi, you guys want any mickies or roasted marshmallows?" Stella asked her friends.

"No way! Our daddy cooked hamburgers outside, and Mama made her pasta salad. I could not eat another thing. Where should we put the blanket?"

Stella walked over to the riverbank for a clear view of the opposite shore.

"How about right here? No trees are in the way. Is it okay with you if the twins join us? My mom asked me if I could keep an eye on them for the fireworks."

"Sure!" Mannie said.

By the time the blanket was down, and the twins and the girls got situated, the first pops were sounding.

Then, "Thung!" and next, the high-pitched sound of a rocket being launched in the distance.

Seconds later, high in the sky, a "Ka-Boom!" and the entire sky over the water exploded with every rainbow color imaginable!

Lastly, "Crackle-crackle-crackle!" and the sparkles fell in a cascade and lit up the river, so Stella could see the rapids, the dock, and the reflection of the shower of colors on the surface of the water.

The fireworks were so beautiful it almost made Stella cry.

"Oohh, Aaahhh," was all they said for the next fifteen minutes.

She knew it was ending when she could hear The Star-Spangled Banner playing from the Celebration, as multiple umbrellas of colored sparkles scattered across the night sky.

It was over too soon, Stella thought.

* * *

After the fireworks, her mother put the twins to bed, and Stella and her friends sat by the fire, listened to fish stories, and heard jokes that sometimes made no sense.

Stella wanted to talk about the men she saw in the Petting Barn, the ones that mentioned Sid being at Shiflin Mountain this past week, but then thought she better not. Her mother would just get upset that she was not with Harry the whole time.

Harry was spending another night in the tent with his friends, so Stella got her favorite bed on the porch again.

That night, she snuggled under the pierzyna and reviewed the day. This Fourth of July was even better than she could have hoped!

THIRTEEN

Gigging

Stella finished bailing the water out of the ten-foot wooden scow and dried the last puddle with a faded towel her mother had donated for boat cleaning. She set the oars firmly in the oarlocks and jumped onto the dock.

Harry had already mounted a 3-horsepower, metallic-blue Evinrude motor on the back of the boat.

He latched the safety chain to the eyehook that her father had screwed into the boat's back plate.

Stella knew this was important, because last year a man in the Fish Camp hit a rock because he was going too fast, and his motor jumped off the boat. As luck would have it, the water was only about ten feet deep and the current wasn't very strong, so they were able to dive in, tie a rope around the motor, and pull it up.

Harry told Stella sometimes, even if you drown an outboard, if you can get it out quick, and get it started, it will dry out and be okay.

But he also said if you lost it down by the bridge, where the current's strong, and the water's eighty feet deep, you're buying a new one.

Stella stood on the dock, hands on her barely noticeable hips, and admired her job. This scow was the boat her father always used for gigging because he had permanently attached a flat board about three feet high at the bow of the boat.

This was where he would hook the Coleman lantern tonight when he, Harry, and Stella went onto the river to spear eels.

At the beginning of summer, she had painted this boat, inside and out. The outside was a bright-pumpkin orange, the color of all her Daddy's rental boats. And inside, a light gray, so it would look clean and not get as hot.

After Stella had painted the outside and inside, Harry coated the bottom with a black gooey tar, and they let it sit in the sun, upside down, for days until the shiny black coating was hard as brick.

* * *

Stella left the dock and climbed the wooden stairs. At the top, she turned to look at all the orange boats tied and waltzing in a circle because of a slight breeze. She smiled to herself, and went into the Cabin, slammed the screen door of the side porch, and walked into the kitchen where her mother was preparing dinner.

"Stella, come help me get supper together so you can get on the water as soon as it gets dark. I'm making city chicken, stewed cabbage, and mashed potatoes. How does that sound?" Stella rubbed her stomach and made yummy noises.

She walked over to the table. "Want me to peel these potatoes?" Her mother smiled and nodded approval.

She was sticking cubes of lean pork and beef onto six-inch wooden sticks, the size of a pencil. After she had made about two dozen, she dipped them in beaten egg with pepper and flaky green spices and coated them with breadcrumbs.

Then she browned them all over in a fry pan and transferred them to her favorite dark blue roaster with the white speckles, put on the cover, and stuck it in the oven to cook slowly for about an hour.

When they were done, you could eat the tender city chicken like a drumstick, and it didn't have any bones!

After Stella peeled and cut up the potatoes, she put them in a pot to cook. She took the lid off a big stewpot simmering on the back burner and inhaled the smell of her mother's stewed cabbage.

Sophie always added lemon juice for the sour and sugar for the sweet. Stella liked to mix cabbage and creamy white potatoes. Her mouth was watering.

"Stella, will you set the table and then wake up those two monsters, please. After swimming up at the island this morning, they zonked out right after lunch. Now they won't want to go to bed tonight, especially with you and Harry out there with Dad."

* * *

Sophie looked out the kitchen window and saw the light-blue panel truck bumping down the dirt road, a cloud of dust trailing behind.

"Oh, good timing. Here come Daddy and Harry. I wonder how they made out at the new spot Daddy found to dig those lampreys. That poor boy, digging in that sand, he won't have a back left by the time he's twenty."

Stella set the table, woke up the twins, and took them outside to see what their father and Harry had dug.

Stella had only gone for lampreys with him one time. As much as she usually liked going with her father for bait, she really did not like lamprey digging at all.

You have to walk pretty far from where the truck is parked and go through a lot of bushes and tall grass to get to the edge of the river or creek.

Stella was worried about snakes the whole time. Then her father would go out into the water, sometimes up to his thighs, and shovel a big pile of sand up onto the bank. Stella would rake her hands through it to find the wiggly lampreys, grab them with a handful of sand, and throw them into the bucket. They had to be about two inches long to be good bait, but sometimes you could get them double or triple that size.

These eels came in two kinds. One didn't bother Stella at all because the mouth was shaped like a fish. It was the American lamprey eel.

The fish book called them elvers when they were small. But everyone at the Fish Camp called them "lampers." The fishermen went crazy to have them because they're the best bait in the river.

You always caught something with lampers. They would pay as much as three dollars a dozen! Stella thought they must be nuts.

But occasionally, her father would throw up a shovel of sand, and when Stella raked through it, there'd be that other blue eel Stella hated.

It had a mouth like a sucker. Sometimes Stella would see a huge dead one in the river. Her father said they would actually stick themselves to a fish and kill it. Stella hated to pick them up, afraid they would stick to her.

Another fishing bait that Stella helped to catch for her father were clippers. She didn't mind catching them.

Their real name is a hellgrammite, and they look ugly because they are deep brown in color, can get up to four inches long, with a switch on their tail.

Their body has segments with tiny feet on the bottom. Their mouth is big, and they have pinchers. If you let them bite you with the pinchers, you are going to feel it.

But they aren't poisonous. Clippers are actually larva of the dobsonfly. Stella often wondered how something as graceful as a winged dobsonfly could start out as such an ugly creature.

To catch them, you have a small wooden frame with chicken wire on the bottom and set the end of the box against shallow rapids, so the water flows through.

Then you pick up rocks in front of the box and wipe off anything on the bottom of the rock. That is where the clippers live until they are ready to molt.

One problem is that you cannot put more than one clipper per container because they will attack and kill each other.

So, once you catch them, you have to put them in their own little container to store. Stella's mother saved all the baby-food jars because they were just the right size.

But Stella remembered the one fisherman that had a huge head of hair, and he would put the clippers into his cap and on his head when he went fishing.

Stella thought he must be nuts too! In general, she thought all fishermen were pretty weird.

* * *

Harry was pulling a bucket out of the back of the truck when Stella walked up with the twins in tow.

"How did it go, Harry? See any snakes?"

"Oh, we did good. I dug four dozen myself, but my back is killing me!" He rubbed the small of his slender trunk. "I saw one humongous water snake! He swam right past me in the creek. I think I peed in my pants, and that scared him away!"

He smiled a wide grin and started to drag the bucket toward the cellar door.

"Hey, Superman, let me help. Stosh and Elsie, you sit right there on that picnic bench until I get back."

Stella and Harry carried the bucket filled with sand, water, and squirming eels to the top of the cellar and down the steps into the cool dark room where their father kept all the live bait for sale.

The clippers were lined up in their baby food jars along the ledge of the foundation, but lampers went into a shallow, open barrel halfway filled with sand covered by water.

Harry and Stella dug into the bucket, caught all the eels in there, and put them into their new home. Their father kept an air pump in the barrel so the eels could get oxygen.

Heck, Stella thought, *they had about a hundred dollars' worth of bait in that barrel for those crazy fishermen!*

"Wow, Harry, how much is Daddy giving you for the four dozen lampers you dug?" Stella was curious to know.

"He said three dollars! I get seventy-five cents per dozen, and he sells them for a dollar and a half. That's not too bad. What do you think?"

Stella looked straight into her brother's gray eyes. "I think it is great! But I don't want to do it. Going in those creeks gives me the creeps. If Daddy offered me five dollars a dozen, I still don't want to do it. I'm going to stick with catching clippers and night crawlers for my spending money."

"Look, Stel," Harry slapped his sister on the back. "Daddy needs the clippers and night crawlers too. Don't worry about it. I heard Ma say that she didn't want Daddy taking you out there for lampers anyway. She said it wasn't something a girl should be doing. It's a guy thing."

Stella did not like what Harry had to say, but all she could muster for a response was a "Humph," and she stomped up the cellar steps.

As soon as she got to the top step, Stella heard Peppy yelping and saw the twins were both lying on top of him, trying to hold him down.

"Stan-ley! Elsie-Marie!" Stella yelled to the twins. "Leave that dog alone! You're lucky he didn't bite you, and you would have deserved it if he did."

They jumped up when they heard her, and Peppy, freed, ran to the back of the Cabin.

"You won't be getting any dessert tonight if I tell Mama. Now go in the Cabin; wash your hands and get ready for supper." She opened the screen door and pushed them through.

Her father was putting away shovels and hip boots in the shed.

"Stella, can you sweep out the back of the truck for me? Then we'll be done with this mess. We've got enough lampers now to get us through a few weeks."

"Sure, Daddy." Stella got the long broom from the shed and headed for the panel truck. "Mama's about got supper ready, and Harry and I put all the lampers in the barrel. They look good!"

"Yeah, we hit on a good spot today. Will try it again in a couple of weeks. And I smell that supper!"

Stella added, "Oh, and the boat is ready. All we need are the gigs and the lantern. Harry already filled the motor with gas and checked the oil. Hope tonight is a good night for spearing!"

Her father looked upward at the clouds. "It should be. The moon is about gone, and there are enough clouds to hide any light we get. And the wind's not bad, so we should be able to see the bottom." He headed to the porch and went into the Cabin.

Stella cleaned the truck with the broom and then went over it with a wet towel. One last check and she slammed the barn doors of the truck, put away the cleaning stuff, and went into the Cabin for supper.

* * *

By the time supper was eaten, and dishes washed and put away, the sun had set.

"Well, Fred, I guess you guys are about ready to get on the water." Sophie looked at him stretched out on the floral-print sofa in the living area of the Cabin. Fred was listening to some news on the radio and digesting Sophie's excellent supper.

"It sounds like they may have a vaccination for this polio disease, Sophie." He sat up on the couch and listened to the report.

Sophie sat down next to him. "You know they closed the pool in town because there were more cases of children that got the polio. Eleanor told me when I called her earlier this week."

"They say it comes from contaminated water but we should be safe here. The river is clean." Fred added.

He swung his feet onto the floor, put on, and laced up his boots.

"Soph, it wouldn't take much to talk me outa gigging, but I know these kids want to go. So, I guess we'll head on. Probably won't stay out too long. Maybe get a dozen or so eels and a couple of bullfrogs."

"We will go up by the island and Cove and swing around the other side of the river. Then we'll motor upstream to come back. Should be back by ten-thirty or so. If not, you can come looking, okay."

"Make sure they wear their lifejackets, Fred. I want ALL of you coming back!" Sophie opened the door leading to the side porch.

The twins were sitting on the glider, finishing their dessert of ice cream covered with their mother's canned blackberries. Stosh was licking the inside of his dish.

"Well, I can tell you liked your dessert, Stosh. Give me those bowls, and let's get on jackets. We'll sit on the swing outside and watch them out on the water for a while."

She collected the dishes, found jackets for the twins, and sat them on the swing near the outside campfire.

There were still a few coals smoldering from last night's fire, so Sophie stirred the ashes around with a stick and added a couple of twigs, and then some small branches and logs, until the fire was burning brightly again. This would help keep away the mosquitoes, she thought.

* * *

Stella's father had filled the Coleman lantern with fuel and pumped it as much as he could.

Then he lit it and settled the flame. Stella could do this, but not very well, and she admired her daddy's skill.

He led the way with the hissing lantern, as all three walked down the stairway at the bank, single file. Harry had two gigs, each a different size of tine, and Stella took up the rear, swinging the empty gray ten-gallon bucket.

When they got to the dock, their father attached the lantern to the hook at the front of the boat. When Harry and Stella got in, he unhooked the bowline and pushed the boat off into the night's black water of the river.

"Stella, now we want you to row very slowly, no splashing with the oars. Harry and I will watch for eels. When we see one, I'll tell you, and you'll need to slow down the boat by back rowing; okay? So just head out toward the Cove and stay as close to shore as you can without scraping bottom. We don't want to get stuck out here in the dark."

"Okay, Daddy, just let me know when you see one."

Stella turned the boat to face upriver and put the oars into the water as smoothly and quietly as she could. This was the first year her father had agreed to let her go spearing, and she was not going to mess this up.

"Dad, there's one!" Harry whispered, excited. "Over to the right. Stella, go a little to my right and slow down."

Stella back rowed a bit and turned the boat slightly. Harry prepared his spear, and in a few seconds, he stabbed it into the water, turning it on the rocky bottom to make sure the eel was gigged.

"I got him, I got him!" Harry shouted, but in a whisper.

"Okay, Harry, just bring him into the boat. Scrape him off on the inside rim. He can't jump out."

Stella's father helped Harry guide the spear into the boat and extract the eel, which now squirmed unhappily beneath the boat seats.

Stella thought the eels were going into the bucket, so when her father said, "INTO THE BOAT," she jerked her feet up into the air. "They won't bite, will they, Daddy?"

"Nah, you don't have to worry about that. Just keep your feet up against the seat if it bothers you." Her father sounded a little tired.

As an afterthought he said, "You did good on that rowing. That's just the speed we need."

The dark water was calm, and the lantern hissed as Stella rowed slowly upriver to the Cove. Harry gigged another eel, and her father speared a large-mouthed bass that happened to be snoozing in the shallows. When they got to the mouth of the Cove, the rocky bottom turned sandy.

"Stella, aim towards that shallow area so Harry and I can jump out." Her father directed Stella.

He pulled the bow of the boat onto the sand and unlatched the lantern.

Harry grabbed the gray bucket and told his sister, "Stella, you stay here in the boat. We're going to walk along this side of the Cove and look for bullfrogs. You won't be afraid, will you? We won't be long."

Stella said she'd be okay, but she didn't mean it. She saw the light from the lantern growing dim as they moved further away from the boat, and she was left sitting in the boat in total darkness, with eels squirming under her feet.

Stella thought the bullfrogs along the shoreline must have been having a convention, because they were so loud, she could barely hear anything else. Fireflies were everywhere, and now and then close by, a huge fish would break the surface.

After a few minutes, Stella's eyes started to get used to the darkness, and she could see outlines of the bushes and trees around her.

There was a path from the Cove to a house that sat on the riverbank above them. The family that owned the cottage was not here during July, but Stella thought she saw a light flickering in one of the windows.

For a second, she thought she saw a shadow cross the light! She rubbed her eyes to see if it was only her imagination. She looked at the window again, but the light was gone. Stella heard Harry and Daddy's voices in the distance.

Was it really a light? Was it really the shadow of someone in the house? Good grief, could it be One Hand Sid?

Stella remembered a prayer cousin El had taught her to say if she was ever afraid.

Dear sweet angel, full of grace, keep me safe in this strange place. She repeated it several times aloud, until the prayer and her own voice quieted her fear.

It wasn't long before the light from the lantern got brighter and brighter, and Daddy and Harry were back at the boat.

"Hey, I see One Hand Sid didn't get you." Harry laughed and got into the boat. "We gigged about six bullies, good size."

"Well, there are enough bullfrogs, as you can hear!!" Stella shouted into Harry's face.

"Okay, you two. Stella, it is your turn to spear a couple. Harry, take us to the island, and let's see what's there. Stella, come up here and settle yourself on the seat. Kneel on that boat cushion, but first let me push us off."

Her father hung the lantern on the bow hook as he pushed the boat back into the river and hopped in.

Stella did a hundred-eighty degree on her butt with her feet still in the air and pointed herself toward the front of the boat. Then she kneeled on the cushion, grabbed the spear, and held it tightly in front of her.

"Now I want you to look ahead in the water. You'll see the eels lying on the bottom. Sometimes they take the shape and color of the rocks, so you have to look sharp. Give Harry enough time to slow down, too."

Stella could not believe how clear the water was. She didn't expect the bottom to look so clear. By the light of the lantern, she could see every detail of the rocks and algae and even minnows.

Here and there, small fish frozen by the light broke their trance and darted away.

"There, Daddy, there. Is that one?" She spoke in a hushed voice, pointing to a wiggly shadow on the bottom.

"Yes, that's a nice-size eel. Harry, slow it down; it's to your left. Stel, get ready, and when you gig him, kind of turn the spear back and forth to make sure he's gigged. I'll help you get him in the boat."

Stella was shaking, the spear was shaking, the entire world was shaking, as far as she could tell.

But just as Harry slowly rowed the boat to the spot, she stabbed the spear into the rocks, and she could feel the resistance. She could tell the eel was fighting back, but she turned and turned the spear until Daddy made her bring it back up.

"Don't torture him to death, young'un.' Now bring him in the boat."

She pulled the snaky, squirming eel out of the water and scraped him off on the inside rim of the boat. Let Harry worry about him now, she thought.

She was still shaking, but Daddy was saying she had done an excellent job. *Boy, gigging was really hard work.* Stella took a deep breath.

"Hey, Stel, I think that one is bigger than all the ones I gigged; darn it!" Harry laughed and turned back around to row the boat.

Fred motioned to his son, "Harry, row up around the point of the island, into the rapids side of the river. Eels like hanging out in faster running water sometimes. Let's see if Stel can get a few more there. But stay close to the island, so the water's not so rough."

Harry guided the boat around the tip of the island, and he struggled to keep the boat pointed in the faster running water. In a few minutes, Fred tugged at Stella's shirt and pointed to the left. "There's a good-sized one. Let's see if you can get him."

Stella got her spear ready. She wasn't as nervous this time.

She squinted her eyes to focus them better, and just as Harry moved the boat into position, she stabbed at the water.

She barely caught the end of the tail, and her father had to spear the head of the eel with his gig. Together they brought the creature into the boat.

"Well, now that's teamwork, right?" her father said. Stella just smiled and was relieved she hadn't lost it.

"Okay, see if Harry can find a few along the other side of the river." Stella carefully climbed back into the rowing seat and positioned her feet above the floor.

There were eels squirming everywhere now. It was like a snake pit. But she focused on the river in front of her and listened for directions.

She rowed the boat away from the rapids and into quieter water along the shore across the river from the Fish Camp.

Lights were on in most of the cabins, and Stella could see the outline of her mother and the twins, sitting on the swing in front of the fire.

Several renters had joined Sophie by the fire, and Stella could hear them laughing. She almost wished she were there instead of in the boat. But, so far, she hadn't messed up. Her father didn't yell at her even once.

She maneuvered the boat between two big rocks, and Harry gigged a big eel right there. The light started to fade, and Daddy had to pump up the Coleman again.

The current was helping Stella row the boat downstream, and sometimes she had to back row to slow it down enough.

Soon they were in the wide eddy before the bridge. The water was getting very deep, even close to shore. It was too deep to gig.

Fred maneuvered his way to the back of the boat, started the motor, and crossed over to the other side of the river.

"I think we should motor back now. We got a pretty nice catch tonight. Agreed?" Their father asked them.

Harry sat in front, and Stella stayed in the middle seat.

"Sounds good to me," was Harry's reply.

"This was really fun," replied Stella, stated like she meant it.

As they passed Indian Rock Ledge, Stella reminded them about what happened a few years ago. "This is where Mama thought she saw a drowned baby, right?"

"It sure is. I guess you won't ever forget that story, huh." Her father slowed the engine, and he stared in the water as if looking for a particular spot.

As the boat approached the dock, Fred shut off the motor, and Harry hopped out and tied the bowline. He unlatched the Coleman, let Stella hop out, and together he and his father gathered up all the eels into the bucket.

Stella wondered how the bullfrogs felt about that kind of company. Her father took a bail can and drew a few cans of water from the river and washed down the inside of the boat to get rid of the slime from the eels. Stella knew she would have to clean it tomorrow.

Together they climbed the stairs to the Cabin. Her mother had already put the twins to bed, and she was sitting alone on the swing by the fire.

Stella could tell she looked relieved they were back, and she looked a little lonely and tired.

"Well, how'd you do? Sure looked like you were spearing something out there."

Harry dropped the bucket in front of his mother. "Look here. I'd say we did all right! I'm going to go clean these now. Want to help, Stel?"

"Sure, I'll give it a shot." The back-porch floodlight shined onto the outside sink against the Cabin, so they could clean eels there.

Their father had put up a board with a nail in it. With his sharp knife, Harry circled an eel's tough skin below its gills and then hung its lower jaw on the nail.

Then, with needle nosed pliers, he skinned the eel in one swoop. Stella cut off the heads, gutted, and rinsed each eel.

Together they skinned and cleaned all fourteen eels in less than thirty minutes.

Harry said he'd take care of the bullfrogs in the morning, put them in a container, and tossed them in the fridge on the porch.

Stella and Harry carried the bucket of cleaned eels to the swing where their parents sat.

"We're done. Want me to put them in the fridge or freezer, Ma?"

Sophie got up and picked up the bucket. "I'll put them in the fridge. We can have them for lunch tomorrow if you want. There is a container of city chickens left. Want me to heat them up and bring them out?"

"You don't even have to heat mine," Harry said. "I'll eat them cold. I'm starving!"

"I'll help, Mama." Stella grabbed the bucket from her mother, and together they went to the kitchen. When Stella and her mother came out with a tray of warmed leftovers, her father had put more sticks of wood on the fire and was sitting on the swing next to Harry.

A stick popped and sparks flew into the black sky. A breeze was blowing up from the water.

Fred pushed against the ground with his foot, and the swing squeaked its familiar tune.

He said, "Well, I'd say this is the life. How 'bout you?" Harry looked over at his dad, nodded, and smiled.

FOURTEEN

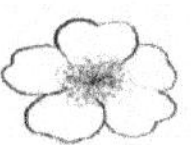

Going to Church

"Harry, are you ready?" Stella yelled to her brother through the door to his make-shift bedroom on the porch.

"Mama said we won't be able to do confession before Mass if we don't leave now." She drew out the "now" word.

Stella heard scuffling in Harry's room, and in a few minutes, he burst through the door, slicking down a blonde cowlick. He scowled at his sister, tromped past her, and headed for the bathroom.

Over his shoulder he shouted, "I'll be ready in a minute" and slammed the bathroom door shut.

Stella watched all this attitude, shrugged her shoulders, and yelled through the bathroom door as she passed, "I'm going to the car, Mr. Crabapple!"

Her mother had backed the car near the porch with the twins in the back seat. They were playing "scissors, rock, paper" and slapping each other playfully.

Stella hopped in between them. "Stop that you two or I won't bring you a treat from town." The twins immediately got quiet.

Harry pushed open the back porch door and jumped into the front seat. "Sorry, Ma, I overslept. I guess cleaning all those eels last night did me in."

Her mother just groaned and turned her eyes skyward.

"Do you two have money for the collection at church?" She put the car in gear and pulled out of the backyard and up the dirt hill to River Road.

"I've got a quarter for each one." Stella felt the outline of the coins against her jacket pocket. "The second one is a special fund collection for the Gannett's; to help them with the fire damage I think."

Harry fumbled through his pockets, "I'm good too."

Sophie stopped at the top of the dirt hill and put the car in neutral. She scrounged through her purse and handed Stella a dollar bill over the front seat.

"Stella, put this in the second collection for the Gannets." She put the car back in gear and turned left onto River Road toward town.

After another left turn onto the Darbytown Bridge over the river, the car rumbled over the bridge deck with its metal ridges.

From this viewpoint, Stella could see the airport on her left. All the July Fourth concessions were gone and the hanger where Stella saw "the gangsters" was shut tight. She shivered with the memory of them.

On the right side of the bridge there was a huge eddy that narrowed into shallow rapids downstream that caused fishermen so much trouble if they got too close.

The small village sat on the other side of the bridge. It was basically a one street town that circled the community.

There were a half dozen stores, the Post Office, and a lumberyard at the edge of town.

But today her mother went straight past the main street and continued up the hill to the tiny Catholic church on the opposite side of town.

Sophie pulled into the parking lot and Stella and Harry jumped out. "Stella, don't forget your mantilla." Her mother handed Stella a triangular, lacey head covering. This was a requirement for all females to be worn in church.

"And make sure you behave, and be careful walking back, especially over the bridge. I don't want to come looking for you or fishing you out of the river."

"Bye Harry, bye Stella, don't forget our treat," the twins sang from the back seat as their mother pulled out of the church parking lot to head back home to the cabin.

Stella and Harry hurried up the front steps of the white-washed church. The worn, wooden doors were open and gave welcome to a tiny vestibule.

Stella dipped her fingertips into a clam shell held by an angel and blessed herself with the holy water.

Inside the church there were a dozen rows of wooden pews on either side of the center aisle.

The confessional was on the left side corner at the back of the church and Stella and Harry headed towards it.

Stella stood in line, waiting for her turn to enter the tiny cubicle. Within a few minutes Lola emerged from the darkened confessional doorway and smiled when she saw Stella. She motioned to a pew and headed in that direction.

Stella entered and closed the door behind her. She knelt on a soft cushion and noticed a small ray of light sneaking through a crack in the door.

It was still very dark, quiet, and smelled of incense. Then she heard the screened window in front of her slowly slide open.

With head down, she stated "Forgive me Father for I have sinned. My last confession was two weeks ago."

A very gentle voice whispered back through the window. "And what sins have you committed, my child?"

Stella took a deep breath and started her confession, "I argued with my brother, about five times; I was jealous of my friend's new outfit; I swam in the deep water when Mama told me not to; I sneaked the last cookie; I lost patience with the twins and yelled at them, many times."

Stella wanted to mention the men she saw in the hanger at the July Fourth Picnic Celebration but decided against it.

She had also missed going to church last Sunday because of all the activities at the Cabin and wondered what Sister Gerry would say about that. But Stella didn't really think it was a sin.

"Hmm, my dear child," the same gentle voice whispered through the darkened fabric screen, "You must remember to obey your parents and honor your family and friends. Say five Hail Marys for your penance. God be with you."

Stella saw the dark outline of the priest motion the sign of the cross with his hand through the shadowed curtain and heard the window close.

Whew, she thought as she opened the cubicle door and was struck by bright light from the stained-glass windows flanking the sides of the church.

She was feeling grateful that the confession was over and walked over to the end of the pew where Lola and Manny were sitting. After they high fived, she dropped to her knees and made the sign of the cross.

Harry was the last person to enter the confessional so when he came out of the cubicle the priest also left and slipped through the door at the front of the church to dress for the service.

Harry found the pew that Chi-Chi had already secured and joined him there.

Stella put her head down in the pew and recited her penance, then sat next to her friends.

She loved this church. The purple granite church at home was huge and had beautiful stained-glass windows and gold trim everywhere. This church was simple.

There were only four stained-glass windows on either side and the altar was just a wooden table with cloth over it.

Stella wondered whether God listened to your prayers any differently depending on the size and beauty of the church.

Sometimes Stella felt the closest to God when she sat in her rowboat drifting down the river and listening to the cowbirds or the wind rustling through the trees.

She came out of her daydream when the church bells rang loudly, and the service began.

* * *

As the recessional psalm was sung, everyone exited the church. After passing Father Munie and receiving his blessing, all the fish camp kids started walking down the hill toward town.

At the bottom of the hill, right before the bridge crossed the river, the group turned and entered a small variety store. It had a soda shop with red cushioned stools, and everyone picked a spot.

Stella's treat was a frosted mug of real root beer and a bar of Wyler's black licorice.

She bought two rolls of Necco candy for the twins and stuffed them in her pocket.

After their treat, the group left the store and started their walk over the bridge.

"Chi Chi, do you see that whirlpool down there, right in front of that huge wall of rock?" Harry pointed to spot of black swirling water near the edge of the rock wall. "My dad said they've lost a few people in it."

Chi Chi added, "Do you know the water's over one hundred feet deep under the bridge? That's why they call it "The Narrows."

Just then a car drove over the bridge, and they could all feel the bridge shaking and rumbling under their feet.

"Wow, can you feel that!" Lola sped up her walk to the other side. At the end of the bridge, they turned right onto River Road again. They passed the guard rail where they always waited for their father on his way from the city to the Cabin.

Huge butternut and oak trees shaded the narrow road, and they came upon the "Haunted House." A three-story wooden building stood out on a small hill. Victorian filigree decorated the eaves and ancient trees were scattered amongst the property.

"Harry, I can't believe you guys actually went into that house. Weren't you scared to death?" Stella grabbed Lola's arm in a tight squeeze.

"Yeah, that was a pretty thrilling experience, as I remember." Harry looked over at Chi Chi and snickered. "We were lucky to get out alive."

"We didn't think there was anyone living there so we found our way up into the attic and saw lots of strange stuff."

Chi Chi then added to the story. "Things from another country, or planet, for sure! Then we heard someone walking in the house and got our tails out of there in a flash."

"Not sure what goes on in there." Harry and Chi Chi shook their heads in disbelief and started punching each other in jest as the group ran down the road.

They all sang "I love to go a wandering above the clear blue skies" and jogged down River Road.

When they got to the spot where you could see Lola and Manny's cabin below the road, the girls hugged their goodbyes.

Lola and Manny climbed over the guardrail where they could take a shortcut down the mountainside. It was a very steep set of wooden stairs their father had built but saved them a lot of time.

"Bye everybody." Lola and Manny waved to Stella and the guys and Lola asked, "Hey Stel, are you going swimming at the Island later?"

"That sounds like fun. I'll check with my Mama and let you know. Bye." Stella waved and ran down the road to catch up with Harry and Chi Chi.

The guys interlocked their arms with Stella, and they sang their way back to the Cabin.

Earlier that week, Stella overheard her parents saying this was turning out to be a good summer from the business end. It made Stella feel like the Cabin might be saved.

What a very special summer, so far.

FIFTEEN

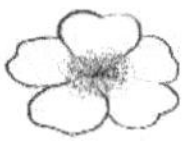

Hurricane Terror!

In the middle of August, Stella walked into the living room on a Thursday morning. Sheets of rain pelted the picture window facing the river. The radio blared storm warnings and the most recent position of Hurricane Diane.

Sophie and several of the renters sat around the pedestal table in the main Cabin. Stella plopped herself on the couch next to Uncle Joe.

"Mama, are we supposed to GET this Hurricane?"

Stella was trying her best to understand the weather report. "Shhh, Stella. We are trying to figure that out," her mother whispered.

A man's deep voice was reporting, …and Hurricane Diane is now moving through the eastern part of Pennsylvania, dumping a half dozen inches of rain in areas already saturated from the last hurricane, Connie, which roared through the same area only days ago. Looks like we are in for a double whammy!"

One of the renters got up from the table and nervously ran his fingers through his hair. "Sophie, I think we are going to try to head home as soon as we can get packed. This storm sounds bad, and we don't want to take the chance of the river overflowing the bank, with Laura being pregnant, and all, you know."

The tall slender man sounded truly apologetic. Dan and Laura had been regular customers for three years and were supposed to rent one of the cabins for another week. Stella knew her mother would have to give back next week's rent.

But there was nothing they could do, and you couldn't blame them. They hugged Sophie and left the Cabin to go pack their belongings.

The report continued, … "serious flooding is expected, and persons living in low-lying areas are strongly advised to move to higher ground. Rivers and creeks are expected to overflow their banks. The worst of the wind and rain will hit the area this evening and throughout the night."

Sophie looked out the window and shook her head. "Harry is moving the boats further up the bank again. The dock is already under water. Joe, are you and Bettie going to leave, too?"

"Nah, Sophie, I think we'll ride it out with you and the kids. We'll just have us a real hurricane party; what do you say, sweetheart?" He tussled Stella's hair, and she knew he was just trying to reassure her and her mother.

"I think that's great, Uncle Joe." Stella knew Joe was really a cousin, but they all called him Uncle Joe anyway.

She added as an afterthought, "We have plenty of candles, and Harry has his Channel Master radio in case the power goes out. We'll be just fine, right here."

In a little while, a door slammed, and Harry sloshed into the room. He took off his wet yellow slicker and hung it on the door. His mother handed him a towel to dry off.

"Please put those soggy sneakers on the porch," Sophie pleaded to Harry.

"Roger, Ma." Harry came back from the porch and pulled up a chair at the table. "Man, the river rose two feet since this morning. I tied all the boats to the cable near the top of the bank. Ma, we have another six to ten feet of leeway. I sure hope we don't need it!"

"We just heard a weather report, and this storm sounds serious," Sophie told Harry. "They are advising everyone to go to high ground. I am going to try again to see if I can get through to Dad."

Sophie went into the kitchen and came back in a few minutes. She looked worried to Stella.

"I couldn't get through. Guess the storm has already knocked out the telephone lines. I hope Dan and Laura can get back home."

"Ma, I left a motor on one of the boats just in case I have to go out there and tow somebody." Harry looked out the picture window and scanned the dirty roaring water. "There's unbelievable stuff floating down this river!"

"If this water gets much higher, we need to move those Adirondack chairs away from the bank," his mother replied. "I just paid twenty dollars for them and don't want them floating down the river." Sophie looked over at Stella.

"Don't forget to remind me later, Stella."

* * *

All afternoon, Stella watched parts of people's lives float past her. Tables and chairs, barrels, parts of docks and fences all paraded down the river. She even saw a whole chicken coop, with the chickens still inside, moving rapidly downstream.

Stella was scanning the river with the binoculars when she saw something upriver in the rapids. "Harry, look, isn't that a dock with two boats still tied to it, and it's heading this way? Do you think we can we save them?"

Within a few minutes, Harry and Stella grabbed their rain jackets, ran out of the Cabin, and launched their scow before their mother realized what they were doing and could stop them.

"Boy, Harry, I have never seen the current so fast! And you can't even see the bottom!" They motored their way out to the runaway dock.

Harry handed Stella his knife, and she cut the boats free of the dock and tied the lines to cleats on the scow. They couldn't save the dock. It was too heavy and moving too fast in the current.

That was the last rescue their mother would allow, and she made Harry take the motor off the boat and store it in the shed. Then he tied all their boats to the walnut tree at the top of the bank and crossed his fingers.

It rained, thundered, and blew harder; bolts of lightning slashed the sky at regular intervals. Stella stared out the picture window. Her beautiful river was now a dark and deadly churning power.

The electric went out in the afternoon, and darkness came early. Suddenly Stella remembered and yelled to her mother, "Mama, the chairs. We forgot about the chairs!"

Sophie let out a groan, grabbed her slicker, and headed outside.

"Mama, please don't go. It's not safe!" Stella yelled. "You forgot the flashlight!"

"Don't worry, Stella," her mother called back as the screen door slammed behind her. "Stay with the twins. I'll just drag the chairs closer to the Cabin."

Stella grabbed the flashlight and shined it through the picture window, trying to give her Mama light as best she could.

Just then, a brilliant flash of lightning lit the sky, and Stella saw her mother hovering over a precipice. One of the Adirondack chairs had already been washed into the river, and the other was teetering on the ledge above a newly formed, roaring stream.

The overflow from River Road above the Cabin had cut a watery path alongside the Cabin and into the river. One more step and her mother would follow the chair into the water. Stella was terrified that her mother would be swept away.

"Harry!!!" she screamed. "Mama's going to drown!" Harry and Stella ran to the door and struggled for a moment to get through it, each trying to get out to save their mother.

When they reached her, she was hanging on to a root, the water pulling at her, trying to take her into the river.

"Grab her shirt, Stel. Ma, give me your hand. Now let go of the root so I can pull you up." Another flash of lightning stabbed the sky, and Stella could see the fear in Mama's eyes.

She grabbed her mother's slicker and pulled as hard as her own body could stand, and then more, until she and Harry hauled their mother safely to solid ground. Tears and rain mixed on Stella's face as mother, son, and daughter hugged on the edge of Stella's beloved riverbank.

* * *

Uncle Joe and Aunt Bettie stayed in the Cabin with Stella's family for the rest of the night. The Barconis and Zulachs were now isolated from the rest of the Fish Camp by the newly formed stream, but after yelling back and forth, the adults confirmed everyone was okay.

Candles and flashlights flickered like fireflies throughout the night. Eventually, the time between lightning strikes got longer, and they could hear only distant rumbling of thunder.

Peep frogs, first only a few, but then in chorus, bravely sang again.

* * *

The sun was already up when the familiar blue bakery truck bumped down the dirt road into the camp. For the first time in Stella's life, her father seemed overwhelmed. He hugged their mother in a way Stella had never seen, and Stella saw tears in his eyes as Harry told him about the rescue.

Stella knew what would happen next. All the customers for the rental cabins cancelled their reservations for the rest of the season.

They either were victims of the hurricane or did not want to be in a hurricane-ravaged area. Polio was a disease connected with contaminated water, and people were afraid to swim or fish in the river after a hurricane.

To Stella, this meant all the progress made on the loan for the Cabin would be lost. Her parents would have to refund the renters' deposits.

By the time her father arrived, the river had already gone down a few feet, leaving behind a high-water mark of trash. It lined the riverbank on both sides, like a dirty bathtub ring after the plug was pulled.

Harry and his dad kept moving the boats as the water receded. The men in the Fish Camp got wooden planks and made a temporary bridge across the new creek that had nearly drowned Sophie, so the Barconis and Zulachs could have a way out of the camp.

As Stella was scanning the river with the binoculars, she noticed a bright-colored object downstream on the riverbank.

"Harry, look at that blue thing by Indian Ledge. You think that's one of Mama's Adirondack chairs?" She handed him the binocs.

"Sure enough! I'll put a motor on the scow and go down and get it. At least one will get saved."

The power company restored the power to the Fish Camp area late that afternoon. With Fred there, Uncle Joe decided they should head home, so now all the rental cabins were empty.

That night was a quiet dinner. Their dad told how he had tried to get to the Cabin, but all the roads were flooded, and the bridge in Coalville was washed out. He had to take a roundabout way until he found a bridge he could cross.

Stella wanted to ask what would happen now, with all the renters gone, but she already knew the answer.

The owner of the two boats they had rescued came by and gave Harry ten dollars for saving them. Harry just handed the money to his dad.

"Daddy, how long will it be before the river cleans up?" Stella asked.

"Not sure, Stel, probably about two weeks." He knew why she was asking. "We might see some folks here for Labor Day weekend, if the weather holds."

* * *

That night Stella knelt by her bed and thanked God, and the Blessed Mother, and her patron saint, St. Lucy, for saving her mother. But she also prayed, selfishly she knew, for something to happen that would save the Cabin.

SIXTEEN

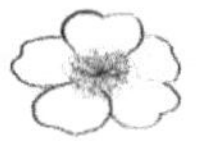

Bad Makes Good

The next weekend, Sophie insisted that Fred bring Helen, Stella's best friend in the city, with him to the Cabin because Stella seemed so depressed after the hurricane.

Stella looked for her father's truck all afternoon. When she saw it pass above the Cabin, she ran so fast, she reached the top of the road just as the blue truck was going to make the turn.

"Helen, Helen, I'm so glad to see you!" Stella jumped up and down. When she opened the door of the truck, Helen slid out.

After a long hug, they walked arm in arm down the dirt path, following the truck's trail of dust.

"Helen, you look skinny! Did you stop eating, or what?" Stella moved away from her friend and noticed the change in Helen's shape.

"Yeah, I lost twenty pounds this summer. My mother took me to this doctor, and he said it was not healthy for me to weigh as much as I did, so they put me on this diet. No more banana splits, which, as you know are my favorite food!"

"Well, you look great! So, catch me up on all the news. Is Barb still chasing after Eddie?"

Stella made a face, then listened to Helen tell her about the July 4th dance at the Church and who had a crush on whom.

"How did you make out with the hurricane, Stel? We were really worried about you folks up here. How bad was it? Were you scared?"

Helen pressured Stella for details, but Stella couldn't tell her everything. There were parts of the hurricane experience Stella knew she would not resolve for a long time. Finally, she changed the subject.

"Helen, tomorrow I arranged for you to meet a special friend. Now, let's get you unpacked. Harry said we could have the porch bedroom this week. You will love it! At night, you can hear the frogs and the river and see the fireflies, and there's always a cool breeze. Oh, I am SOO glad to see you!"

After Stella hugged Helen again, they went into the Cabin.

Sophie made city chicken for dinner because she knew Helen liked it. When Stella told her mother about the weight Helen had lost on her diet, she added another vegetable to the table and put the bowl of mashed potatoes next to Harry.

Instead of the lemon meringue pie she had baked, Sophie served a bowl of fruit salad made with handpicked blackberries and blueberries, fresh cantaloupe, and watermelon.

"Helen, tomorrow I'm going to take you to see Misty, the white horse I wrote about in my letters. And guess what?" Stella looked straight into Helen's face.

"Well, what, Stel? What is the surprise?" Helen looked at her friend anxiously.

"Misty's owner, Suzanna, went on vacation this week with her family, and she asked me to take care of Misty and Sully, AND she told me we could ride them if we wanted to.

So tomorrow, you get to go horseback riding!

"Wow, Stel, but I've never ridden a horse in my life!" Helen seemed a bit overwhelmed with this news.

"OH, don't worry. Sully is the best-behaved horse in the world. She would follow Misty anywhere, and we will stay off the main roads."

"Now Stella," her mother was listening to the plan and had her own opinion of it.

"I do not want you taking any chances with those horses, you hear me. No galloping down River Road. Helen is not used to those animals like you are."

"No problem, Mama. We'll take it nice and slow." Stella turned and smiled at Helen.

The next morning Stella and Helen were up by seven. Stella told Helen to be sure to wear jeans and sneakers. They ate a quick breakfast and headed to the barn.

As they started walking down the path to the barn from River Road, Misty must have heard them because he came out and trotted along the fence. But Sully just stood at the entrance to the stall and nickered to the girls.

"See how smart they are. They know it's time for breakfast. After I feed them, we can brush them before we ride." Stella opened the gate and let Helen through.

Stella put a quart of steamed, rolled oats and a capful of vitamins in Misty's feed bucket, and Misty whinnied the whole time she was preparing it, stomping his front feet, anxious to get breakfast.

Sully got a slightly smaller portion of oats, since she was older and smaller. She also had better manners than Misty and stood to the side patiently while Stella filled her bucket.

To Stella it almost seemed as though she nodded a thank you before she moved her body towards the bucket and started to eat.

"Aren't they beautiful, Helen?" Stella laid her head on Misty's shoulder and took a deep breath. "They smell so good to me; hay and oats, and horsehair!"

Helen went over to Sully and patted her neck, then tickled her underbelly. When the horse shivered, the girls laughed. "I think Sully's ticklish, Stel."

After the horses finished their meal, Stella tied them to the crossties, and she showed Helen how to currycomb the neck and shoulders and rump.

"You never use a curry comb on their face or legs, though, Helen, because their skin is too tender in those spots. Always use the soft bristle brush." Stella picked up a yellow brush with fine hair and showed her friend how to gently brush around the eyes and down the horse's legs.

"Now, for the hard part." Stella showed Helen how to stand close to the horse and pick up each foot, holding the bottom of the hoof up. With a hoof pick, Stella dug out the shavings and dirt until she cleaned the familiar V shape, or "frog." Then she gently released each foot.

"Helen, you must stand really close to the horse when you're doing this, because if the horse tries to kick away, they can't build up enough force to really hurt you. Suzanna said sometimes they kick out of reflex, not really trying to hit you."

Stella and Helen got the tack from the barn and saddled up the two horses. Stella left Misty on the crosstie and walked Helen around on Sully, making sure she felt comfortable enough to leave the paddock.

"Stel, Sully's so sweet!" Helen said. "I feel really safe up here."

"Good. Let's ride!" Stella unsnapped Misty from the crosstie and opened the gate. She had to walk Misty next to the fence, so she could stand on the rail to get up on the horse. Misty was very tall. Then both girls walked the horses out to the path.

"Helen, let's go out to River Road and take the first field to the right." Stella and Misty led the way.

They walked the horses along the edge of the fields bordering the river and stopped to watch a swooping red hawk and a woodchuck. Stella was in heaven, riding with her best friend.

In a straightaway, Stella told Helen she was going to trot Misty, and she did. But when she stopped and turned around, she saw Sully trotting along, trying to keep up.

Helen didn't know how to post, so she was jostled up and down, like a Jack in The Box. She had a tight grip on the horn of the saddle. Stella knew Helen would have a sore butt tomorrow. They did not trot after that.

"Helen, let's cross River Road here, and take the logging path I know. Suzanna and I have been on it earlier this summer and it's pretty, going through the trees. Follow me."

Stella made her way to the road and stopped. She looked both ways and listened carefully to hear for any car or truck that might be down the road. Then she told Helen to follow, and they crossed the road and entered a path in the woods.

"Wow, the hurricane washed out a part of this road. Let's see how far we can get."

Where dead trees were lying across the path in a few places, the girls had to maneuver the horses around them.

They were about a half-mile from the road when Misty started to act strange. He seemed nervous and jumpy, snorting as if something was frightening him.

"Helen, I have never seen Misty act like this. Maybe there's an animal around here we can't see."

Misty just stopped so suddenly that Stella had to grab onto his mane just to stay in the saddle. Misty shook his head and would not budge.

Stella scanned the path ahead and finally realized what the horse saw.

Lying in the gully alongside the logging path was a crumpled-up form of a body. A tree had fallen across it. Stella could see shoes, pants, and hair. And when she breathed in, the air smelled rotten.

Stella tried to scream, but she could not. She turned Misty around and motioned to Helen to turn. Then they made their way as fast as the horses could safely go, out to the road.

"Stella, what was there? What did you see?" Helen was scared.

"Helen, it, it was a body, I think. Did you smell it? We've got to get help. Just try to keep up with me as best you can."

Stella broke her own rule and her promise to her mother, and galloped Misty along River Road, this time hoping a car would come along.

Sully tried to keep up, and Helen just held on tight. Galloping was a whole lot more comfortable than trotting, she found out.

They passed the fields, and the barn, and kept on going until they reached the Fish Camp.

Sophie saw them barreling down the road and came running out of the Cabin, calling "Fred, Fred, something's wrong!"

Fred ran out of the cellar and grabbed Misty's reins when Stella stopped in front of him. In a few minutes, Sully and Helen came up behind them.

"Daddy, Mama!" Stella could barely talk because she was out of breath. "We were on the logger path about a mile from the barn, and I saw a body there, in dark clothes, in the gully. And it smelled really bad! I got so scared."

Harry and Lester ran up from the river when they heard Sophie scream. His dad told them to help with the horses, and he would call the sheriff. In a few minutes he came back out and said the sheriff would be there in about ten minutes.

Stella knew the horses were breathing heavy, and she was worried about Sully, so she told Helen to walk her, and she walked Misty to cool them down.

"Harry, can you get us a bucket of water to give the horses once we cool them down. I do not want them to get sick, and Suzanna said never to give a horse any water until it had been walked and was not breathing heavy."

About the time Stella was watering the horses, the sheriff's car bumped down the Fish Camp Road and pulled into the driveway.

"Morning, Fred, Sophie." He tipped his hat to Sophie and turned to look at Stella and Helen. "What did you gals see out there?"

Stella spoke up. "Mr. Sheriff, I think it's a dead body; well, I know it's dead, for sure, because it smells awful." Stella was trying her best to explain.

"And it was lying in the gully alongside the logger road. Maybe it washed out of a grave or something," she added.

"Humph," the sheriff stroked his chin, thoughtfully. "Don't know of anyone being buried in that area, and don't know of anyone missing, you know, that's unaccounted for."

He turned to Stella's father. "What say we go take a look, Fred?"

Fred nodded and walked to the sheriff's car, then turned around. "Sophie, better follow the girls back to the barn in the car in case they meet up with traffic.

Harry, you stay near the phone in case we want to call you."

"Roger, Dad." Harry nodded.

Sophie rounded up the twins and followed Stella and Helen back to the barn. They rode with loose reins and let the horses walk at their pace the entire time.

Stella felt a little calmer now, but the picture of the body stuck in her mind and the smell in her nose.

At the barn they put away the tack, rinsed off the horses, and used the sweat blade to dry them. Then Stella gave each of the horses an extra-large helping of hay and locked the gate. Her mother waited in the car with the twins.

"Sorry about breaking my promise to you, Mama. You know, about galloping on River Road," Stella truly sounded sorry, and a little bit worried about the consequences.

"Honey, I am just so glad to have you both safe. I hope the sheriff can figure this one out." She put the car in gear and headed back to the Fish Camp.

Just as they reached the turn to the Cabin, a Pennsylvania State Police car with flashing lights passed them in the opposite direction.

Another dark-colored van followed, and Stella noticed a name on the side of the door—CORONER. She was not sure what Coroner meant, but knew it had to do with the body in that gully.

About an hour later, the sheriff's car pulled into the driveway. Fred got out, said something to the sheriff, slammed the door, and waved. The car backed onto the road and went up the hill.

Harry and Stella ran to meet him. "Did you find the body? Who was it? What do you know?" Stella fired one question after another.

"Okay, Stel, stop the questions for a minute. We have interesting news. Let's all go in the Cabin, and we'll talk about it."

When Sophie saw the sheriff drop Fred off, she put the twins to bed for a nap and promised them double dessert if they stayed in the bed until she came to get them.

Word spread quickly through the Fish Camp. Several of the men came to the Cabin to hear first-hand what was going on. Harry, Lester, Helen, and Stella sat next to her father at the pedestal table, waiting.

"Well, we went down the logger road, just like you told us. We could definitely follow the horses tracks and could see right where Misty made his standoff. And sure enough, there in the gully were the remains of a body." Stella shuddered as she remembered the scene.

"It looks like the body either was washed into the gully from somewhere in the woods or that tree fell on him as he was going down the gully. It probably happened during the hurricane because the body was there about a week or so."

"The dark van that passed you coming home was the Coroner. He will take the remains to the morgue at the hospital and will let us know when he finishes the autopsy. It was a male, and one other thing was noticeably clear." Daddy looked around the room, then said, "The body was missing the right hand."

"The Shooter!" Lester whispered what everybody else was thinking. "Stella, you found One Hand Sid! He really did exist!"

Stella did not know whether to cry, or laugh, or just scream. Instead, her jaw dropped, and she didn't utter a sound.

"Well, Stel," Harry commented after her silence. "I believe this is the first time in my life I've ever seen you speechless."

Harry's words broke the spell, and everyone laughed, not because the situation was funny, but just as a release of the tension.

"Now, we can't draw any conclusions to this, you hear," Fred was talking again. "They have a lot of work to do to confirm whose body this is. But there is one more interesting fact we found up there."

Everyone again focused on Fred's next words. "The sheriff found a small sack in this guy's pocket when he was looking for some kind of I.D. In it was some jewelry, including a whopper of a ring, a little dirty, but then diamonds clean up well."

This time he smiled and said to Stella, "Good job, Stel, in Hitting the Jackpot! And I think Misty deserves a special treat."

* * *

Stella's picture appeared on the front page of the local paper. She was sitting on Misty, reins in hand, and the barn in the background.

The owner of the diamond ring sent a telegram "Attn: Stella Karvotsky" to thank her for returning the family heirloom. But more important to Stella than the attention was the reward for finding the lost treasure.

Although she did not understand a lot about what money could buy, her father told her the reward was enough to pay off the bank note for the Cabin and to buy a new truck. There might even be enough to get her mother a new wringer washing machine and to start a small savings account for Stella's college education.

All these things were great to hear, but the main reward to Stella was she would still have the Cabin.

Thank you, God.

SEVENTEEN

Labor Day Weekend Goodbyes

Strong strokes, left arm, right arm; *keep kicking, stay focused on the shore ahead, fight the current that wants to take me downstream, I can make it!* Stella told herself.

Harry was somewhere behind her. She could hear the oars splash into the water. He encouraged her, "Go Stella, you can do it, you're almost there."

She did not have to look back to know that her mother was watching. She hated the water and couldn't swim but was willing to let Stella take the challenge of swimming across the whole river for the first time.

Everyone in the Fish Camp knew who had swum the river. It was a rite of passage. Harry and Chi Chi did it two years ago. Her mother said she could try.

The current wasn't pulling as hard now. Stella still couldn't touch the rocky bottom, but her arms were aching, chest hurting; she dog paddled as a kind of rest.

Harry shouted again, "Come on, Stel; don't give up!" Stella again stroked left and then right until her big toe stubbed a rock.

"Oh, that hurt" she said to herself, but the green shore was so close.

Finally, she was able to stand up. Arms in the air, Stella turned to look at her mother on the other side and yelled, "I made it, Mama! I made it!" Harry jumped out of the boat next to her and splashed her. "You did it!"

* * *

Stella sat on the swing under the walnut tree. Her shorts felt damp from the early morning dew. She woke up before everyone else to spend a little time alone with the river.

Today was Labor Day, and they would leave to go back to the city. Tomorrow was the first day of sixth grade. Stella was excited about school, in a way, but her heart ached at leaving the Cabin.

She knew she would always remember this summer! It gave her some of her happiest memories, swimming the whole river for the first time, riding Misty and Sully with Suzanna and Helen through the fields and along River Road.

But there were also the saddest moments of her life, as she remembered her favorite horses, Tom and Ginny, dying in Mr. Gannett's burned-down barn.

Stella was reliving the hurricane's scariest moments, when the porch door squeaked open, and Harry came out, yawning and stretching his long slender limbs.

"Hey, Stel, thought I'd find you out here." He sat down on the swing next to his sister. "Looks like Dad and Ma are sleeping in."

"I'm not surprised." Stella rubbed her belly. "That was some cookout last night! I'm still full of that BBQ chicken."

Harry leaned back in the swing and shook his head. "The food was great, but the music was over the top! I didn't even know Mr. Barconi could play the accordion."

"Or that Mama and Daddy could dance the polka like they did!" Stella added.

"Yeah, it was a terrific way to end the summer." Harry got up and used a broken hot dog stick to stir the embers from last night's fire.

"Mannie says her dad plays in a polka band in the valley. He is pretty good." Stella situated herself in the middle of the swing and pushed herself into the air.

"You know, Harry, I was just thinking this summer was amazing. First, we nearly lost the Cabin to the bank, and then nearly lost it to Hurricane Diane!"

"And nearly lost Ma too!" Harry broke in. He threw the broken hot dog stick into the fire. "That was too close for comfort for me. Thank God for that lightning strike!"

Stella stopped the swing, got up and shivered as she remembered her mother hanging on to the tree root in the rushing water.

"Harry, I think at least everything is pretty much back to order. I heard Daddy tell Mama that the bank is satisfied. It makes me feel good to know we were able to help."

Stella sat back down on the swing. "Mama and I will be leaving with the twins after lunch. The good news is she told me we are coming back one weekend in October to celebrate Uncle Josh's seventy-fifth birthday!"

Harry walked over to the swing. "Yeah, Dad said he was planning to invite a bunch of the locals and do it up right. Move over." Stella moved from the middle to make room and Harry sat next to his sister.

"You know, Harry, I'm kind of looking forward to school this year, but I sure am going to miss being here."

"Oh, the winter will go fast, and before you know it, we'll be back, painting boats and picking night crawlers." Harry laid his head back and closed his eyes.

"And next summer, I get to fly!"

RECIPES

For more recipes, please check the website www.stellascabin.com.

Sophie's Polish Apple Cake

1-1/2 cups Mazola oil
2 cups sugar
3 eggs
1 tsp vanilla

Blend oil, sugar, eggs, and vanilla.
Add and blend together:
3 cups regular flour
½ tsp salt
1 tsp baking soda
1 tsp baking powder

Finally, add and gently blend:
4 cups peeled and diced McIntosh apples
1 cup chopped walnuts
1 cup chopped maraschino cherries

Fill a greased and floured tube pan and bake at 350 degrees for 1-1/4 hours or until toothpick inserted in cake comes clean.

Carol Lunney-Hampson

ACKNOWLEDGMENTS

With great appreciation and thanks—

To my friend and fellow writer, Ed Hall who encouraged me and constructively critiqued and edited my revision of Stella's Special Summer, which was published in 2015,

And to my New Bern Writing Group for their valuable suggestions,

To my family for supporting each other as our parents would want; in the process we keep our story alive,

To Marv Josaitis for his flattering review and helpful comments, even in the last days of his earthly life,

To Mickey Gulino for keeping the concept of the cabin alive, and

Finally, to my best friend and husband, Jim

ABOUT THE AUTHOR

In her professional career, Carol Zalewski Lunney Hampson taught college biology, researched, and published in the field of Electron Microscopy, and spent twenty-plus years working in product development, management, and marketing in the world of pharmaceuticals. Presently retired, she lives on a creek near the historical coastal town of New Bern, North Carolina, with her husband and enjoys writing, gardening, tennis, and sailing.

www.stellascabin.com

QUESTIONS FOR DISCUSSION

1. What is a hermaphrodite? What are the possible evolutionary benefits of this characteristic?

____

____

____

____

2. Why do you think the baby lampreys called elvers were such good bait for fishing?

____

____

____

____

3. What are the stages in the life cycle of the DobsonFly? Where do the "clippers" that Stella and her family picked for bait show up in this cycle? Where were the clippers hiding and how did Stella catch them?

____

____

____

____

4. Did you think that One Hand Sid was in the cabin overlooking the Cove when Stella was sitting in the boat alone in the dark waiting for her father and brother to return from gigging the bullfrogs?

____

____

____

____

5. Do you think it was One Hand Sid walking on the edge of the golf course when Stella was picking nightcrawlers in the dark?

____

____

____

____

6. How do you think One Hand Sid could have been involved in the tragic fire at Farmer Gannett's where Tom and Ginny's lives were lost? Was he responsible?

____

____

____

____

7. Compare the public response to the medical management and treatment of the Polio epidemic in the 1950s to the recent COVID outbreak. Was the public more confident of the treatment for Polio than for COVID? What caused such a change in accepting the treatment protocols?

____

____

____

____

____

____